WILLIAM
SHAKESPEARE'S

MUCH ADO
ABOUT
MEAN GIRLS

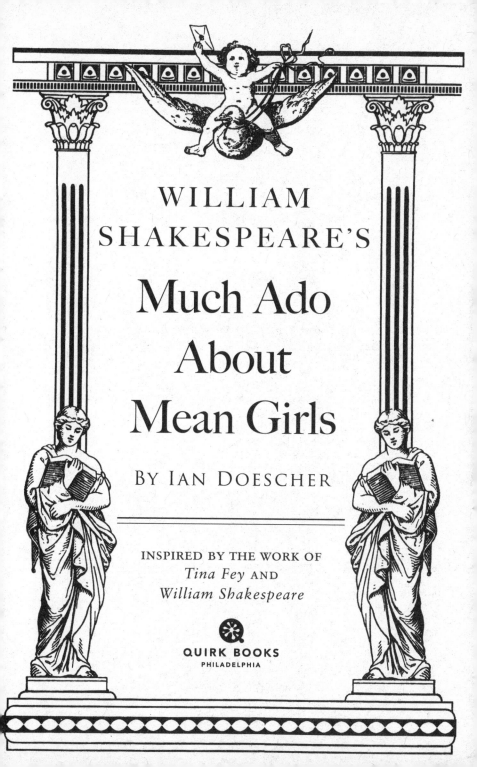

WILLIAM SHAKESPEARE'S

Much Ado
About
Mean Girls

By Ian Doescher

INSPIRED BY THE WORK OF
Tina Fey AND
William Shakespeare

QUIRK BOOKS
PHILADELPHIA

For Tom and Kristin,
meanest girls I know

A Pop Shakespeare Book

MEANGIRLS

Library of Congress Cataloging in Publication Number: 2018943044

ISBN: 978-1-68369-117-4

Printed in Canada

Typeset in Sabon

Designed by Doogie Horner
Text by Ian Doescher
Interior illustrations by Kent Barton
Cover illustration by Ana San José Cortajarena
Production management by John J. McGurk

Quirk Books
215 Church Street
Philadelphia, PA 19106
quirkbooks.com

10 9 8 7 6 5 4 3 2 1

A NOTE ABOUT
THE SERIES

Welcome to the world of Pop Shakespeare!

Each book in this series gives a Shakespearean makeover to your favorite movie or television show, re-creating each moment from the original as if the Bard of Avon had written it himself. The lines are composed in iambic pentameter, and the whole is structured into acts and scenes, complete with numbered lines and stage directions.

Astute readers will be delighted to discover Easter eggs, historical references, and sly allusions to Shakespeare's most famous plays, characters, and themes, which you can learn more about in the author's Afterword. A Reader's Guide is also included, for those who want to learn more about Shakespeare's style.

LIST OF ILLUSTRATIONS

WILLIAM SHAKESPEARE'S
MUCH ADO ABOUT MEAN GIRLS

DRAMATIS PERSONAE

CHORUS

CADY HERON, *a young woman*

LADY *and* SIR HERON, *her parents*

REGINA GEORGE, *a shrewish young woman and leader of the Plastics*

GRETCHEN WIENERS, *a troubled young woman and member of the Plastics*

KAREN SMITH, *a doltish young woman and member of the Plastics*

JANIS IAN, *a cunning young woman*

DAMIAN, *a kindhearted young man*

AARON SAMUELS, *an attractive young man*

MADAM SHARON NORBURY, *a wise teacher*

SIR RONALD DUVALL, *a beleaguered school principal*

LADY GEORGE, *Regina's mother*

COACH CARR, *a teacher of health*

KEVIN GNAPOOR, *a math enthusiast and bad-arse deejay*

SHANE OMAN, *a brute*

KRISTEN HADLEY, JASON, TAYLOR WEDELL, SETH MOSAKOWSKI, LEA EDWARDS, TRANG PAK, BETHANY BYRD, DAWN SCHWEITZER, SUN JIN DINH, *and* TIM PAK, *students*

LADY WEDELL, *a troubled parent*

VARIOUS STUDENTS AND TEACHERS

PROLOGUE

Evanston, Illinois, in the New World.

Enter CHORUS.

CHORUS   When audiences 'round the globe appear,
Desiring stories of a woman's fate,
Our playwright answereth the calling clear,
Preparing ample banquet for your plate.
This tale of lasses takes us unto school   5
With many shrewish girls and boyish asses,
Wherein they make mistakes and play the fool,
And learn hard lessons far beyond their classes.
To this fey story make I introduction—
Which shows us Cady Heron's youthful age—   10
Her narrative unfolds in our production
In these few hours upon our simple stage.
I, prologue-like, your humble patience pray,
Gently to hear, kindly to judge, our play.

[Exit.

ACT

I

SCENE 1

At the Heron residence and North Shore High School.

Enter CADY HERON *and her parents,* LADY HERON *and* SIR HERON.

SIR H.   Proceed, young Cady, to procure thy lunch,
And by the bite of it end woes and all.
There ne'er was situation so enflam'd
That by a meal was not made easier.
Within this bag shalt thou a dollar find,   5
With which thou mayst buy milk an thou dost wish.
Ask thou the bigger children where 'tis done
And, by my troth, they'll gladly give thee aid.

LADY H.   Remember'st thou the number of thy home?
Take this along; I writ it for thy sake.   10
I prithee, place it in thy pocket safe—
If thou dost love me, thou wilt lose it not.
[*Aside:*] I'll seem the fool I am not; Cady, strong,
Will be herself. [*To Cady:*] Art thou prepar'd for
school?

CADY   E'en were I passing wise, like Seneca,   15
I'd not have readiness as on me falls.

SIR H.   A picture ere thou leavest home I'll take,
That we, one day, recall this moment rare.
[*They take a photograph together. Exeunt Lady
and Sir Heron as Cady walks to school.*

CADY   'Tis natural, methinks, that parents cry
Upon the day their child first goeth schoolward.   20
Perforce this is the case most typical

When children are a meagre five years old.
I am sixteen and was, until today,
School'd by my parents in our fam'ly home.
Good gentles, like a waiting, open book,   25
The content of your minds is plain to read:
"A homeschool'd child is th'utmost rarity,
An 'twere a freak one would in circus find."
Your minds, belike, imagine instances
When children taught at home are strange, indeed.   30

Enter CHILD I *above, on balcony.*

CHILD 1   The spelling of the short word xylocarp—
A fruit that hath a husky, woody shell—
Is plain: X-Y-L-O-C-A-R-P.
                 [Exit Child 1.

CADY   Or, mayhap, ye assume we hold a faith
Bizarre and dangerous in the extreme.   35

Enter CHILD 2 *above, on balcony.*

CHILD 2   Upon the third day of creation, God
Hath made the Remington bolt-action rifle.
For "Lo," God said, "my people must have aught
With which to fight the mighty dinosaurs
And—ages hence—the homosexuals."   40
Amen say I, and all my family.
                 [Exit Child 2.

CADY   Think not with prejudice upon my state,
For, truly, normal is my family.
Though, in this case, 'tis normal temper'd by

The occupation of my parents two: 45
They both are researching zoologists,
Who spent the last twelve years on Afric plains.
My parents did know more of snakes than sneakers,
More knowledge of the zebras than of Zen,
More happy near the lions than Detroit,   50
More calm upon safari than in Chrome.
My life was wonderful beyond compare,
As I did grow among the pleasant beasts
And ev'ry day enjoy'd the open air.
It was a joyful, satisfying life,   55
Until my mother earn'd a teaching post
At old Northwestern University,
Complete with tenure—forcing our return.
Farewell said I to Afric and its plains,
And bid hello to high school and its pains.   60

> *[She is nearly struck by*
> *a passing bus as she crosses a street.*

Alas! I must be careful, by my troth—
Ne'er was a day in Africa so fraught.

Enter many STUDENTS, *including* JANIS IAN,
   DAMIAN, *and* KRISTEN HADLEY.

Behold, such varied students on display,
Array'd in current fashion, in such clothes
As I have never own'd in sixteen years.   65
Shall I attain the grace and confidence
With which my striking peers comport themselves?
The crowd is quick and unpredictable—
Balls fly from yonder, faster than a cheetah,

Then soar like eagle thither on their way.   70
The students roughly bump and jostle like
A herd of antelope at water's edge.
Nearby some boyish scoundrels light a pyre,
As if some ritual they did enact.
So new and so mysterious—O wonder!   75
How many goodly creatures are there here!
How beauteous mankind is! O brave new world,
That has such people in it! Now, to class.

> [*Exeunt most students as Cady walks into her*
> *classroom. Janis, Damian, and other students sit*
> *at desks. Cady mistakes Kristen for her teacher.*

Here is the teacher—tall and self-assur'd:
I'll speak to her and introduce myself.   80
[*To Kristen:*] Holla, I know not if you heard of me.
My path hath newly brought me to this school,
Where I shall be your student: Cady Heron.

KRISTEN   An thou dost ever speak again to me,
A painful kick unto thine ass I'll grant.   85

> [*Cady begins to sit.*

JANIS   Sit not upon that seat, or thou shalt be
In trouble with one Kristen Hadley—she
Whom thou didst think was teacher unto us—
For her small boyfriend shall assume that seat.

Enter KRISTEN HADLEY'S BOYFRIEND,
sitting next to her and kissing her.

KRISTEN   Hello, diminutive red-headed love.   90

> [*They kiss. Cady looks for another seat.*

JANIS   Did not I speak the words and prove them true?

	Sit not there, either, for the boy in front
	Is flatulent beyond all remedy.
GASSY STD.	[*aside:*] O shame, to have a reputation thus!
	I am for gas renown'd, but hath a soul 95
	That longeth for a song compos'd of words—
	Say I: hail, poetry! Thou heav'n-born maid,
	Indeed, thou gildest e'en the farter's trade.
CADY	Shall I no seat within this classroom find?

Enter Madam Norbury, *knocking into* Cady
and spilling coffee on herself.

NORBURY	Hello, all—O, alack!
CADY	—Apologies! 100
NORBURY	Nay, set thy heart at rest. 'Tis not thy fault.
	My fortune doth run low in muck and mud—
	My life's quaint mazes in the wanton green
	For lack of tread are undistinguishable.

[*She begins to remove her jumper
on which she spilled the coffee.*

Enter Sir Duvall.

DUVALL	Good Madam Norbury, is't well with thee? 105
NORBURY	[*to Cady:*] My undergarment clingeth to my jumper
	And presently my navel's on display—
	'Tis true?
CADY	—Indeed.
NORBURY	—Start to a perfect day.
DUVALL	This is a scene most inexplicable.
	Is ev'rything all right within thy class? 110

NORBURY   'Tis well, or soon shall be.
DUVALL   —How was thy summer?
NORBURY   I was divorcèd from my husband past.
DUVALL   My carpal tunnel syndrome hath return'd.
NORBURY   Were we comparing woes, it seems I win.
DUVALL   Thou winn'st, forsooth—my sorrow goes with thee.   115
            [To students:] I hither came to bring ye this report:
            A newfound student is within your midst,
            Who did arrive from Afric recently.
                        [Madam Norbury spies a black student.
NORBURY   Thou welcome art!
BLACK STD.   —I come from Michigan!
            Pray, lay not your assumptions at my feet.   120
NORBURY   O, Michigan, a wondrous state indeed!
DUVALL   Her name is Caddy, like the shack of old.
            Is there a Caddy Heron present here?
CADY   'Tis I, whose name alike to Katie sounds.
DUVALL   Beg pardon for the mispronunciation.   125
            Thy case is like my nephew, Anfernee,
            Who doth despise the errant sound of it
            When I misspeak and call him Anthony.
            [Aside:] His anger, though, is nothing next to mine,
            When I bethink upon my sister's choice   130
            To give him such a name as Anfernee!
NORBURY   Thou fresh-fac'd Cady, thou most welcome art,
            And thank you, Sir Duvall, for thy report.
DUVALL   It is my pleasure, Madam Norbury.
            If thou hast need of any little thing,   135
            Or if thou'dst speak about thy situation . . .
NORBURY   My thanks. Perhaps another time when I
            Am not array'd in tunic most transparent.

DUVALL   Indeed. [*Aside:*] She is not wrong, I see it well—
             How pleasant and how shapely is her form.   140
             [*To students:*] Good day unto ye all. Learn well, learn
                                      true.

                 [*Exit Sir Duvall. Exit Madam Norbury
               severally. Janis, Damian, and other students
                  change classrooms as Cady speaks.*]

CADY   My first day in the school pass'd in a blur—
             A most confusing and distressing blur,
             Wherein I was in trouble for such things
             As I had ne'er imagin'd I would be.   145

Enter CHEMISTRY TEACHER.

CHEM.   Where art thou bound?
CADY   —Unto the restroom, sir.
CHEM.   Thou dost the lavatory pass require,
             If 'tis thy plan to thither boldly go.
CADY   I see. Can you deliver such to me?
CHEM.   Thy truancy is plain. Sit thou once more.   150
                    [*Exit chemistry teacher.*
CADY   Ne'er had I liv'd within so foul a world
             Where no adult would trust me or my words,
             And where they spent the livelong day in yelling.

Enter ENGLISH TEACHER, HISTORY TEACHER, MUSIC TEACHER, *and*
GERMAN TEACHER *above, on balcony.*

ENGLISH   Read not beyond the page that is assign'd
             For if thou dost, the words may rot thy brain!   155
HISTORY   The color of thy pen may not be green,

	For history is mark'd by shades of gray!	
MUSIC	There shall be none of foodstuffs in my class,	
	For such behavior strikes discordant notes.	
GERMAN	Nein, bleiben ihren vorgenannten Platz,	160
	Für Deutschland wächst auf ihre Unterstützung.	

[Exeunt teachers.

CADY   My puzzlement did not abate by lunchtime,
          As I no welcome found at any seat:
          One group did make their keen abhorrence known
          By placing their effects where I would sit.   165
          Another talks of things impolitic—
          Aloud they talk'd of women's nipplous parts.
          E'en when I spake the greeting "Jambo!" to
          A group I did assume were African,
          They were perplex'd and did not return the greeting.   170
          While I had friends when I in Afric dwelt,
          Thus far I had not one in Evanston.

[Exeunt all but Cady.

          Inside the restroom I did sit and eat
          To hide bewilderment and loneliness.
          O Fates, who spin our threads, I pray you, speak,   175
          For still 'tis beating in my mind, your reason
          For raising this sea storm against my boat.
          Belike I shall not know the reason why,
          For ne'er did Fate respond to mortal cries.

          Enter LADY HERON *and* SIR HERON.

SIR H.   Thy first day done! How didst thou find the school?   180

[Exit Cady, upset.

LADY H.   This silence doth bespeak a brutal day.

O, have we hurt our daughter by our move?
We had a wondrous life in Africa—
Full often hath she gossip'd by my side,
And sat with me on Neptune's yellow sands,   185
Marking the embark'd traders on the flood,
When we have laugh'd to see the sails conceive
And grow big-bellied with the wanton wind.
Now is she silent and will nothing tell—
Would that our daughter suddenly were well!   190

                                        [Exeunt.

SCENE 2

At North Shore High School.

Enter CADY HERON, JANIS IAN, DAMIAN,
and various STUDENTS, *in the classroom.*

CADY   [*aside:*] The second day I come as sojourner—
            Still shaken, if I were to tell the truth.
                        [*Cady sits next to Janis and Damian.*

DAMIAN   The color of thy hair—is't natural?
            Or dost thou shade its hues with crafty dyes?

CADY   'Tis natural.

DAMIAN   —And gorgeous, by my troth.   5

CADY   My thanks, kind gentleman.
                [*Damian grasps Cady's hair and holds it next to*
                                            his own head.

DAMIAN   [*to Janis:*]   —Observe the tint.
It is precisely that for which I long—
A reddish brown like sunset on a field.

JANIS   [*to Cady:*] This forward fellow here is Damian,
Whose gaiety doth overwhelm his sense,   10
Forever sighing over women's hair.

                 [*A rude student passes by.*

RUDE STD.   Thy wig—of hair most false, as from a horse—
Where hast thou got it, Janis?

JANIS   —From thy mother,
Who hath a hairy chest unnatural,
Which only is surpass'd by her foul face,   15
Most Gorgon-like, with spots and hives and boils,
The itch of which she scratcheth all the day.
Although, I'll warrant scratching could not make
It worse, an it were such a face as hers were.
[*To Cady:*] My name is Janis.

CADY   [*aside:*]   —Sharp of tongue and wit!   20
[*To Janis:*] My name is Cady—pleas'd to meet you both.
I bid ye, can you friendly folk tell me
The place wherein I'll find room G14?

             [*Cady hands her schedule to Damian.*

DAMIAN   Health class on Tuesday and on Thursday, too,
Room G14.

JANIS   —In the back building, yea?   25

DAMIAN   In the back building, as thou sayest, Janis.
It certainly existeth—in the back.

JANIS   We thither shall deliver thee ourselves.

CADY   You two are kinder than the day is long.

           [*The bell rings. Students begin
moving to their next classes.*

DAMIAN   Make way, ye rogues and knaves and listless youths!   30
            A newfound morsel walketh through the halls—
            Hail Cady, mighty lass of Africa!

                              [*Exeunt all students except
                                Cady, Janis, and Damian.*

            Health, Spanish, and advancèd calculus?
            These are the things thou studiest this year?

CADY   Of mathematics am I very fond.   35

DAMIAN   Yet wherefore so?

CADY   —'Tis ev'rywhere the same:
            The rules of mathematics are a constant,
            Wherever in the wide world one doth roam.
            It hath no bound or language but its own,
            The selfsame found in ev'ry town and country.   40

DAMIAN   'Tis beautiful—the lady hath such depth!

CADY   Where is the building unto which ye lead?

JANIS   It hath burn'd down in nineteen eighty-seven—
            A fire for education spark'd the flame.

CADY   Shall we not find ourselves in trouble rank,   45
            If we our classes and our school forsake?

JANIS   O, wherefore would we trouble bring on thee,
            As thou art our new friend and confidante?

CADY   [*aside:*] 'Tis not acceptable, a class to shirk—
            This know I, yet the lass hath call'd me friend!   50
            Forsooth, I've neither the position nor
            The inclination to refuse new friends.
            Belike I ne'er shall learn the lessons that
            Are taught upon today's first class of health.

            Enter COACH CARR *above, on balcony.*

CARR	Whate'er you do when you have private time,	55
	Where'er you roam within this world profound,	
	Remember this: 'tis best to not have sex,	
	Lest pregnancy and death on you befall.	
	Have neither sex with partner standing up,	
	Nor sex in the position missionary,	60
	Have neither sex in canine-style fashion,	
	Nor sex involving mouths or derrières,	
	Have neither sex, and neither have ye fun,	
	Nor heavy petting—this is, also, out.	
	Avow to me ye shall have none of sex.	65
	Now, whosoever shall, take rubbers plenty.	
	[Exit Coach Carr.	
JANIS	[*to Cady:*] Why did thy parents not keep thee at home,	
	Therein thine education to complete?	
CADY	The two would see their daughter socializ'd,	
	Prepar'd to function in the daily world.	70
DAMIAN	Thou shalt be socializ'd anon, I'll wager—	
	A slice of heav'nly beauty as thou art.	
CADY	What dost thou mean? Thou speakest of my mien?	
JANIS	By ev'ry regulation thou'rt enow	
	To give a man a fever by thy look,	75
	An aching burn within his very loins,	
	Infernal passion that shall not abate.	
CADY	Am I?	
DAMIAN	—Enjoy it whilst thou canst so do.	
JANIS	How dost thy spell thy name? Remind me, Caddy?	
CADY	'Tis Cady—C-A-D-Y—by my troth.	80
JANIS	Well, for the nonce I still shall thee Caddy,	
	That thou mayst carry all my fondest hopes.	

Enter REGINA GEORGE, GRETCHEN WIENERS, KAREN SMITH, *and various other* STUDENTS, *aside, in physical education class.*

DAMIAN Behold, within the name of all that's holy,
  The clothes that Karen Smith doth wear today.

JANIS 'Tis fitting that the Plastics share one class 85
  To emphasize their physical perfection.

CADY The Plastics? Who and what are they, I pray?

DAMIAN The teenage royalty who rule the school,
  E'er reigning underneath malicious crowns.
  If North Shore High School were a magazine, 90
  They'd grace the cover with their regal bearing.

JANIS Behold the one with visage blank and dim—
  'Tis Karen Smith, a lass of little wit,
  The dumbest person thou shalt ever meet.
  Last year, kind Damian sat next to her 95
  In English class and bore her foolishness.

DAMIAN The lass hath ask'd me how to "orange" spell.

JANIS The thinnest one is Gretchen Wieners, aye,
  With hair most dark and darker spirit still.

DAMIAN The lass is rich. Her father did invent 100
  The Toaster Strudel that the masses love.

JANIS She is a horrid gossip, who doth make
  It her vocation and amusement to
  Know ev'rything of ev'ryone she meets.

DAMIAN 'Tis, peradventure, why her hair is large: 105
  The secrets she doth carry in her pate.

JANIS The worst—pure evil in a human form—
  Is she, Regina George, of beauty rare.
  Be thou not fooled by the lady's looks.
  She may appear a simple, selfish lass 110

                    With reputation for her wantonness,
                    Who would stab e'en her mother in the back,
                    Yet, in reality, she is far more.
DAMIAN   Of bees the queen, of prides the lioness,
                    Of empires empress, and of states the head.   115
                    The others are but workers in her scheme.
JANIS   Regina George—O, how shall I explain?

                    Enter seven STUDENTS *above, on balcony.*

STUD. 1   Regina George is flawless, verily.
STUD. 2   She hath two handbags come from farthest Rome,
                    By Fendi fashion'd for extravagance.   120
                    Her carriage is a silver Lexus car—
                    A marvelous machine by any standard.
STUD. 3   'Tis said the lady's hair is well insur'd—
                    Ten thousand ducats should it damag'd be.
STUD. 4   She traveleth to Oriental shores—   125
                    E'en to Japan—wherein she doth appear
                    In advertisements for their lavish cars.
STUD. 5   Her fav'rite entertainment's *Vars'ty Blues*,
                    In which she near could have the starring role.
STUD. 6   She one time met John Stamos on a plane,   130
                    Where he declar'd her pretty as the sky.
STUD. 7   One time, my very visage—even mine!—
                    Did have the privilege to feel her punch.
                    'Twas wonderful beyond my wildest dreams.
                         [*Exeunt Students 1 through 7 from balcony.*
DAMIAN   She always hath the direst, fiercest look,   135
                    And e'er is crown'd the queen of Fling of Spring.
JANIS   Of what concern is that?

DAMIAN   —'Tis my concern!
            Each year the senior class prepares a dance
            Made for the underclassmen to enjoy.
            The Fling of Spring—a merry, joyful thing—   140
            And whosoever is elected as
            The queen and king of Fling of Spring shall bring
            An automatic honor on themselves.
            As they assume their rightful place as heads
            Of North Shore's School Activities Committee.   145
            Because I am an active member of
            The School Activities Committee, 'tis,
            I shall admit, a strong concern of mine.

JANIS   What should I do with thee? Dress thee in my
            Apparel, Damian, and make thee, then,   150
            My waiting-gentlewoman? Zounds! Thou art
            As gay and merry as the day is long.
            The gayest army could not thee defeat.
                    [Students begin gathering and sitting for lunch.
            [To Cady:] I have prepar'd a simple map for thee,
            Withal to navigate the North Shore waters.   155
            Where thou dost sit within the dining hall
            Is crucial, for each group doth have its place.
            The freshmen just beside the ROTC lads,
            The preps and jocks of junior varsity,
            The Asian nerds, the Asians cool as ice,   160
            The jocks of varsity—no juniors, they—
            The hotties black who still unfriendly are,
            The lasses who eat feelings more than food,
            The lasses who eat naught and are too thin,
            The people who wish they were aught yet aren't,   165
            The burnouts, band geeks lusty in the height,

The greatest people thou shalt ever meet—
I mean myself and Damian, of course—
And, finally, the worst—beware the Plastics.
        [Janis and Damian sit aside. Regina, Gretchen,
            and Karen sit nearby. Cady obtains food and
                begins moving toward them.

                Enter JASON.

JASON   I beg thee, pardon this, mine interruption.   170
            Wilt thou engage with some few questions, which
            I ask of all new students at the school?
CADY   I shall.
JASON   —Say, is thy muffin butter'd well?
CADY   What?
JASON   —Shall I find a helpful volunteer,
            Who would most gladly butter up thy muffin?   175
CADY   My muffin?
REGINA   —Doth this rascal pester thee?
            I bid thee, Jason, wherefore art thou skeez?
JASON   Nay, merely am I friendly, and no skeez.
GRETCHEN   Thou wert suppos'd to call on me last night.
REGINA   Take heed, young Jason: thou shalt not arrive   180
            Unto a party I do kindly host
            With Gretchen at thy side, to then approach
            This comely ingenue most innocent
            Before our eyes but three days afterward.
            She is not ta'en with thee, canst thou not see?   185
            [To Cady:] Wouldst thou have intercourse with this
                                            foul lad?
CADY   Nay, thanks to thee, though, for the offer.

REGINA   —See?
The matter settl'd is decisively.
Let him that mov'd you hither move you hence.

JASON   Thou churlish, common-kissing pox-mark'd strumpet! 190

                        [Exit Jason in disgrace.

REGINA   [to Cady:] Wilt thou sit here with us? We have the
                                                space.
We would have discourse with thee, newfound friend.

CADY   [aside:] What shall I do when fac'd with this request?
Aside I see sweet Janis motioning
As if to say, "What madness comes o'er thee?   195
Wilt thou be seated with our enemies?"
Yet should I not these women grant a chance,
An opportunity before I judge
Them utterly unworthy of my time?
They may, in some way, be misunderstood,   200
And not the wanton hags describ'd by Janis.
I'll test the Plastics' character myself.

              [Cady sits with Regina, Gretchen, and Karen.

REGINA   Now, tell me, wherefore do I know thee not?

CADY   Unto the schoolhouse am I newly come.
My family and I arriv'd from Afric,   205
Where I was brought up lo these many years.

REGINA   From Afric, didst thou say?

CADY   —Such was my word.
By parents was I homeschool'd ere this year.

REGINA   The words thou speakest stranger still become.

CADY   My mother was a schoolmarm unto me . . .   210

REGINA   Nay, nay—to be homeschool'd is nothing new.
I know the term—I am not daft nor dumb.
What doth perplex is this: hast thou ne'er been

A student at a real school heretofore?

[Cady shakes her head no.

Shut up thy mouth whilst I exclaim! Shut it!   215

CADY   I did not speak.

REGINA   —A homeschool student, eh?

'Tis fascinating, verily.

CADY   —My thanks.

REGINA   Yet still thou dost possess a beauty rare.

Young budding virgin, fair and fresh and sweet,

Happy the parents of so fair a child;   220

Happier the man, whom favorable stars

Allot thee for his lovely bed-fellow!

CADY   Again, my thanks.

REGINA   —Thou dost agree withal?

CADY   What?

REGINA   —Thou think'st also thou art beautiful.

CADY   I tell thee honestly, that such to know   225

Did never meddle with my simple thoughts.

REGINA   By all that is divine, behold thy bracelet—

A stunning piece of jewelry it is!

How didst thou come by such a lovely thing?

CADY   My mother fashion'd it and gave it me.   230

REGINA   'Tis worthy of the public's admiration.

GRETCHEN So fetch it is, it fetcheth ev'ry glance.

REGINA   What is this "fetch" and, pray, whence cometh it?

GRETCHEN A word come swimming 'cross the ocean blue,

From England's ruddy shores. Know'st thou this

country? 235

KAREN   If thou hast come from Afric, why art white?

GRETCHEN Nay, Karen, by the gods—thou canst not ask

A person wherefore she or he is white!

REGINA   Couldst thou, in kindness, give us privacy,
                Wherein we three shall speak a moment, Cady?   240
                              [The Plastics turn aside to speak privately.

CADY   Of course. [*Aside:*] How like three parrots they do seem,
                E'er chattering with naught of substance said.
                Poor Janis yonder, next to Damian,
                Doth signal as to ask what I have done.

REGINA   Before I speak, know this: we are not wont   245
                To do the thing we're bound to do herein;
                This is important, we would have thee know.

GRETCHEN   We kindly bid thee, wilt thou dine with us
                Each day through the remainder of the week?

CADY   While this is kind, I have two friends—

REGINA   —'Tis well,   250
                No further conversation shall we have,
                But we'll expect to see thee on the morrow.

KAREN   On Wednesdays, we array ourselves in pink!
                              *[Exeunt Regina, Gretchen, Karen, and other
                              students except Cady, Janis, and Damian. They
                              walk aside into the women's bathroom.*

JANIS   What fire is in mine ears? What scene was this?
                No glory lives behind the back of such.   255
                The Plastics say thou dost deserve, and I
                Believe it better than reportingly.
                Thou hast been claim'd and thou shalt take thy claim!
                Thou shalt wear pink upon the morrow, yea,
                And make report of all Regina sayeth,   260
                No matter how horrendous, rank, and vile.

CADY   Regina seemeth sweet, if I am honest.

JANIS   Go to! Regina George is far from sweet—
                She is the sourest wench who ever liv'd,

	Who sucketh scum from deepest ocean floor.	265
	Her scornful tongue hath ruin'd life entire.	
DAMIAN	The lass is fabulous and evil both.	

Enter STUDENT 8.

STUD. 8	A lad—be gone, away! Why are thou here?	
DAMIAN	The actor, by my troth, Danny DeVito!	
	Thou art a tiny star in ev'ry sky.	270

[Exit Student 8 hastily.

CADY	[*to Janis:*] Why dost thou hate her so?	
JANIS	—What dost thou mean?	
CADY	Regina—thou hast for her hate profound,	
	More than appeareth normal to mine eyes.	
JANIS	Indeed. What is the question thou dost ask?	
CADY	My question is whence cometh thy contempt?	275
DAMIAN	Regina hath announc'd, in rumor's voice,	
	That our bold Janis was a—	
JANIS	—Damian!	
	I bid thee not repeat her heinous words.	
	Whate'er response I give comes not from hate.	
	Methinks it shall bring wondrous joy and mirth	280
	To ply this innocent experiment—	
	Thou shalt spend time with them and make report	
	Of ev'rything they say and think and do.	
CADY	What shall we speak about? None come to mind.	
JANIS	The products that deliver pretty hair.	285
DAMIAN	Or Ashton Kutcher.	
CADY	—Is he troubadour	
	With jobs performing songs a lot like love?	

JANIS	Please, do it for thy newfound friend—e'en me.
CADY	I shall, because it matters so to thee.
	Dost thou have aught in pink that I may wear? 290
JANIS	Nay, ev'ry piece of mine is gray or black.
DAMIAN	Yea, pink! It is the color of my heart,
	The hue of beauty and of loveliness,
	The rosy shade of sunset in the west,
	The tint of salmon rushing through a spring. 295
	Pink is the pigment of a welcome soul,
	Pink is the cheek that blusheth when in love,
	Pink is the underside of newborn feet,
	Pink is the lush camellia on the bush.
	An thou wouldst deck thyself in luscious pink, 300
	Then Damian shall be thy source and guide.

        [Exeunt Janis and Damian as the bell rings.

Enter MADAM NORBURY, AARON SAMUELS,
   KEVIN GNAPOOR, *and other* STUDENTS.

CADY	Eighth period arrives and I am glad
	To enter math, my fav'rite field of study.
	For mathematics was my mind produc'd—
	'Tis understandable and plain to me. 305
	Naught in a class as this could bring me grief.

        [Cady sits behind Aaron.

AARON	Hast thou a pencil thou mayst loan to me?
	Thou art a wonder if thou dost, kind maid.
CADY	No wonder, sir, but certainly a maid.
	[*Aside:*] O heavens, what a handsome, pleasing lad— 310
	There's nothing ill can dwell in such a temple.
	Just once was my heart smitten as 'tis now!

'Twas when I was a younger lass by far—
His name was Nfume and we both were five.
I told him of my simple, childlike love, 315
Yet he did scorn me, bid me go away.
This moment is far diff'rent from the last—
This lad hast struck me like a yellow bus.

NORBURY Say, Cady, hast thou some response?

CADY   —So cute.

      [Cady realizes she has spoken
         her thought aloud.

Forgive me, madam! *A* sub *n* is equal 320
To *n* plus one and over four.

NORBURY   —Just so!
Well done, well done indeed. Ere ye depart,
Remember all your work to do at home.

    [Exeunt Madam Norbury, Aaron, Kevin, and
      other students. Cady walks home.

Enter LADY HERON *and* SIR HERON, *sitting outside their house.*

SIR H. The second day accomplish'd, by my troth!
How was it? Better than the first, I hope. 325

CADY 'Twas well.

LADY H.   —Were other students kind to thee?

CADY Nay, kind is not the word I would employ.

SIR H. Hast thou some newfound friends?

CADY   —Indeed. Farewell.

      [Exit Cady inside her house.

SIR H. These answers of our daughter are too brief.

LADY H. In brevity of words the lass is chief. 330

        [Exeunt.

SCENE 3

At North Shore High School.

Enter CADY HERON, REGINA GEORGE,
GRETCHEN WIENERS, *and* KAREN SMITH, *seated together
at the lunch table. They each don pink attire.*

CADY	[*aside:*] The Plastics, regal as Victoria,
	Do frighten me, like dark and dreadful wood—
	With rules that hide beyond each rolling hill.
GRETCHEN	I will believe thou hast a mind that suits
	With this thy fair and outward character. 5
	Remember this: no tank top shall be worn
	From one day to the next, two in a row,
	And neither shalt thou wear a pony's tail
	As thy hairstyle, excepting once per week—
	It seemeth thou hast chosen thus today. 10
CADY	[*aside:*] No nat'ral world is this, but some Girl World.
GRETCHEN	We also weareth pantaloons for track
	Or jeans on Fridays only, as if we
	Were Catholic and they our fish to eat.
	Break thou our rules and thou'lt not sit withal. 15
	'Tis not just thee, 'tis law for anyone.
	If I were wearing denim jeans today,
	Belike I would be sitting with the freaks,
	Who draw upon their artboards all the day.
	We take a vote before we shall allow 20
	Another soul to eat their lunch with us—
	This is consideration for the group,

	Pursuing constantly the greater good.
	Thou wouldst not purchase garments from a shop
	Ere thou didst ask thy precious friends to share 25
	Their thoughts on thine appearance.
CADY	—Would I not?
GRETCHEN	Exactly. 'Tis the same rule for the lads—
	Thou mayst believe thou art enamor'd of
	A man, yet find thyself mistaken. See?
REGINA	One hundred twenty calories in all, 30
	And forty-eight from fat. 'Tis what percent?
GRETCHEN	Er . . . forty-eight into one hundred twenty . . .
REGINA	The foods I eat, from now, shall have no more
	Than thirty calories compos'd of fat.
CADY	'Tis forty, verily, a plain equation: 35
	If forty-eight is o'er one hundred twenty,
	It equals x above one hundred, yes?
	Cross multiply to solve for x—'tis forty.
REGINA	Where did you study all this goodly speech?
	It is no matter, I shall dine on cheese fries. 40

[*Exit Regina.*

GRETCHEN	Hast thou met any lads whose look thou lik'st?
CADY	A person in my studies calculus.
KAREN	Who is the man?
GRETCHEN	—I'll wager 'tis a senior.
CADY	His name is Aaron Samuels.
KAREN	—Nay, beware!
GRETCHEN	Alas, the lad is not for thee, I fear. 45
	Thou canst not be the budding paramour
	Of Aaron Samuels. Anyone but he.
	He once was boyfriend unto our Regina.
KAREN	'Twas one whole year the two did fondly court.

GRETCHEN   Poor lady, she were better love a dream.   50
            She devastated was when he did end,
            Last summer, the relationship they had.
KAREN   Methought she, for Shane Oman, sent him hence.
GRETCHEN   Yet irregardless of the situation,
            Ex-boyfriends are but clos'd, forbidden books   55
            For friends to borrow from each other's shelves.
            These are but feminism's rules and mores.
            Fear not, though, Cady, this I promise thee:
            Ne'er shall Regina hear what thou hast said;
            I'll keep the secret lock'd within my head.   60

                                                    [Exeunt.

SCENE 4

At North Shore High School.

Enter CADY HERON, MADAM NORBURY,
and KEVIN GNAPOR, *in mathematics class.*

CADY   [*aside:*] Though Aaron was declar'd beyond my rank,
            Still I may look on him, may take him in,
            And think on him—within my heart the first—
            Perhaps may even share a spoken congress
            With him, as boy to girl and man to woman.   5
KEVIN   Holla, thou art the lass from Afric come,
            Whose brains do multiply her mystery?
CADY   Indeed.

KEVIN   —My name is known as Kevin Gnapoor,
The captain of the North Shore Mathletes team.
We take our arms against a sea of troubles—   10
Competing versus teams from other schools
Throughout the splendid state of Illinois.
We shall add twice as many ducats if
The team doth sport a female such as thee.
Thou shouldst consider joining us. Wilt thou?   15

NORBURY   Thou wouldst be perfect, Cady.

CADY   —Verily.
The opportunity shall suit me well,
Enamor'd as I am of mathematics.

KEVIN   Divide thou not my hopes and dreams in twain—
Take thou my calling card and we shall speak.   20

CADY   [aside:] "One Kevin Gnapoor, math enthusiast
And bad-arse deejay"—such a card to play!

KEVIN   Take thou whatever time to think thou need'st.
We would, this year, have doublets for the team.
Farewell, smart Cady, equal of my mind.   25

     [Exeunt Madam Norbury and Kevin severally.
     Cady walks outside.

Enter AARON SAMUELS *aside, at football practice.*

CADY   There, far afield upon the football green,
Doth Aaron practice with assurèd kicks.
I'll wave to him that he may see the smile
My visage proffers when I see his face.

AARON   Good afternoon, kind Cady. Be thou well.   30

KEVIN GNAPOOR

MATH ENTHUSIAST/ BAD-ARSE D.J.
847-555 2148

Enter REGINA GEORGE, GRETCHEN WIENERS,
and KAREN SMITH *in Regina's car.*

REGINA   Come hither, folly-fallen Cady, come!
           We shall anon unto the shopping mall.

CADY   [*aside:*] Regina, like a doll I never had—
           By name of Barbie with her winsome Ken—
           Is glamorous and elegant sans peer.   35
           I'll go withal to make her favor grow.
                    [*Cady gets in the car with Regina, Gretchen,*
                              and Karen. They begin driving.

AARON   [*aside:*] Another lass is, by Regina, trapp'd
           Into a world of lipsticks, hair, and nails.
           This Cady seem'd far different before—
           Yet now I wonder what the lass shall be.   40
                    [*Exit Aaron. Cady, Regina, Gretchen, and*
                              Karen arrive at Old Orchard Mall.

REGINA   [*to Cady:*] How likest thou North Shore?

CADY   —It suiteth well.
My purpose 'tis to join the Mathlete team.

REGINA   Nay, nay, be not so silly, Cady, please.
'Tis social suicide to join that team
Compris'd of nerds and geeks and dorks and freaks.   45
How fortunate thou art to have we three
To guide thee and to mold thee as our own!

CADY   [*aside:*] What would kind Janis think about this scene?
Belike she would throw back her head and laugh.
Old Orchard Mall remindeth me of Afric,   50
Where beasts do gather near the wat'ring hole
And snarl at one another as they drink.

                Enter JASON *with* TAYLOR WEDELL.

GRETCHEN 'Tis Jason!

REGINA   —Where? Ah, there, I see him now.

GRETCHEN The rogue is in the company of Taylor,
She of the horrid family Wedell.   55

KAREN   'Tis said they are romantic'ly inclin'd.

REGINA   Nay, Jason is not to that strumpet link'd.
He shall not treat thee so, as though he plann'd
To comb thy noddle with a three-legg'd stool
And paint your face and use you like a fool.   60
The scoundrel is a villain and a skeez.
Give me thy phone and I shall set this right.

GRETCHEN Thou shalt not call him—

REGINA   —Think'st thou I am simple?

GRETCHEN Nay, never, wise Regina, on my life.
        [*Gretchen hands Regina her phone. Regina dials
            and brings the phone to her ear.*

REGINA   [*into phone:*] Wedell house, please, upon South
                                                              Boulevard.   65

GRETCHEN   What of the tools t'identify a caller?

REGINA   They are no use when call'd through Information.

                   Enter LADY WEDELL *above, on balcony.*

LADY W.   Hello?

REGINA   —May I speak unto Taylor Wedell?

LADY W.   She hath not hither after school arriv'd.
                    May I ask who is calling and leave word?   70

REGINA   'Tis Susan calling from Plann'd Parenthood.
                    Be sure that Taylor calleth me anon;
                    Her test results have been return'd to me.
                    The matter's urgent—growing more each day!

LADY W.   [*aside:*] O shocking news of teenage pregnancy!   75

                                                    [*Exit Lady Wedell.*

REGINA   Now Taylor is not link'd to anyone—
                    Her mother shall give punishments aplenty.

GRETCHEN   Thy plan and action were completely fetch!

CADY   [*aside:*] Is this the way these lasses make their sport?

                        [*Exeunt Cady, Regina, Gretchen, and Karen.
                                        Taylor's phone rings.*

TAYLOR   [*into phone:*] Good afternoon, sweet mother. How art
                                                              thou?   80
                    I bid thee, be thou calm and yell not so.
                    What words are these thou shoutest in mine ears
                    Of lies, deceit, responsibility?
                    How have I wrong'd thee, mother? What? E'en so?
                    Why speakest thou of pregnancy and whoredom?   85
                    The daughter whom thou dost describe with words

Both slanderous and vile—she is not me!
Let she, then, die defil'd, but I do live,
And surely as I live, I am a maid.
O, life, that mother e'er suspected child—　　90
How did come upon these thoughts so wild?

[Exeunt.

ACT

II

SCENE 1

At the George residence.

Enter CADY HERON, REGINA GEORGE,
GRETCHEN WIENERS, *and* KAREN SMITH.

CADY	[*to Regina:*] Thy house is nicest to the pow'r nineteenth,
	Declare I sans condition or amendment.
REGINA	'Tis lovely, is it not? A palace noble.
GRETCHEN	Be sure thou seest her mother's ample breast,
	By power of physician larger made. 5
	'Tis beauty truly blent, whose red and white
	Nature's own sweet and cunning hand laid on,
	And like two stones they rest, both firm and solid.
REGINA	Sweet Mother? Art thou here?

Enter LADY GEORGE.

LADY G.	—How are my girls?
	Your coming has transported me beyond 10
	This ignorant present, and I feel now
	The future in the instant. Welcome home!
GRETCHEN	Fair greetings, Lady George. May I present
	A new lass come unto our school: 'tis Cady.
LADY G.	Thou sweetheart, welcome to my humble home. 15
	[*Lady George embraces Cady.*
CADY	[*aside:*] The words of Gretchen prove entirely true:
	Her breasts are like two violent batt'ring rams!
LADY G.	If thou hast needs, but ask us. All our service

In every point twice done and then done double
Were poor and single business to contend   20
Against those honors deep and broad wherewith
Thy presence loads our house. Be thou not shy.
There are no rules within this house of mine—
I am no mother regular, forsooth!
A cool mom I, 'tis so, Regina, yea?   25

REGINA   My tongue will tell the anger of my heart,
An thou dost longer speak. Pray, let us go.

LADY G.   A treat for hump day shall I make ye four.

        [Exit Lady George as the others repair to
                                 Regina's room.

CADY   This is thy room, palatial and ornate?
With "princess" writ in gold upon the wall   30
O'er where thou sleepest on thy silken sheets?

REGINA   It once belong'd unto my parents two,
Until I forcèd them to trade with me.
Let us play station ninety-eight point eight.

        [They adjust the radio and
                      a song begins playing.

Dost thou, young Cady, come from Africa,   35
Know who doth sing this song of lutes and lyrics?

CADY   Mayhap the Girls of Spice?

REGINA   *[to Gretchen and Karen:]*—Ha! She is sweet,
Her innocence is brighter than the sun.
Like one who cometh from the planet Mars,
She knoweth little of our earthly customs.   40

KAREN   How large my hips! I would thou hadst my bones.

GRETCHEN   My legs do better understand me than
I wish to look on them—behold my calves!
How like two useless lumps they do appear.

REGINA	At least ye two can wear a halter top— 45
	With shoulders passing mannish, I dare not!
CADY	[*aside:*] Methought, once, there were two forms: slim
	and fat.
	Herein I better learn: there is no end
	Of how the female form may errant turn.
GRETCHEN	My hairline is bizarre.
REGINA	—My pores are craters! 50
KAREN	My nail beds are disastrous.
REGINA	[*to Cady:*] —What of thee?
CADY	My breath is noisome in the morningtide.
KAREN	Eww.

Enter LADY GEORGE *bearing drinks, with her* DOG.

LADY G.	—Happy is the hour from four to six!
CADY	My thanks—yet, is there alcohol herein?
LADY G.	By heaven, nay, what thinkest thou of me? 55
	Am I no mother to a teenage girl?
	Yet, honestly, if thou wouldst have a drink,
	I'd happily provide, an thou shalt have't
	Within my house where I may o'er thee watch.
CADY	Nay, thank you, Lady George.
LADY G.	—'Tis well, 'tis well. 60
	Now, ladies four, what is the four-one-one?
	How do ye spend your days, what is your news?
	But screw your courage to the sticking-place
	And tell me all the gossip that ye know!
	[*Lady George's dog climbs into her lap and*
	begins biting her breast.
CADY	[*aside:*] This is a sight I do not love to look on— 65

	The dog doth sense the forgery of meat.	
LADY G.	What music do ye listen to, what jams?	
REGINA	Pray, Mother, walk aside and fix thy hair!	
LADY G.	I shall. O ladies, how ye keep me young!	
	Yea, I do love ye more than I can tell.	70

[Exit Lady George. Karen pulls the Burn Book
from Regina's shelf.

KAREN	By heaven, O, I do remember this!	
	Was ever book containing such vile matter	
	So fairly bound?	
REGINA	—Not since forever have	
	I thought about that book upon my shelf.	
GRETCHEN	Come hither, Cady, feast thine eyes on this.	75
	'Tis call'd our Burn Book, wherein we do take	
	The images of lasses from the yearbook	
	We have cut from the page with simple snip	
	And writ our honest comments thereupon.	
	Here is one entry from a bygone year:	80

"Trang Pak is but a grotsky little byotch."

REGINA   'Tis true unto today.

GRETCHEN   —"Dawn Schweitzer is
A virgin maid of massive girth, forsooth."

REGINA   'Tis true, at least by half.

GRETCHEN   —Ha, ha, such wit!

KAREN   "One Amber, of the house D'Alessio,   85
Was wont to practice kissing on a hot dog."

GRETCHEN   And this one, simply: "Janis Ian: dyke."

CADY   [*aside:*] Alas, my friend is slander'd here, in ink!
Poor Janis, so abus'd. O, my heart bleeds
To think o'the teen that they have turn'd her to.   90

KAREN   Who is that in the picture, next to her?

GRETCHEN   Methinks he is a lad call'd Damian.

CADY   His gaiety doth overwhelm his sense!

REGINA   'Tis humorous, indeed! Write it therein.

CADY   [*aside:*] How quickly I betray him with these words,   95
Which Janis utter'd as a jest before—
Belike such speech is only suitable
When spoken by a worthy friend like Janis.
Anon I'll tell my friends what I have seen—
This Burn Book tactless, fill'd with spirit mean.   100

                                        [*Exeunt.*

SCENE 2

At the Old Orchard Mall.

Enter JANIS IAN.

JANIS   No kind employment have I in this mall,
           Where all is hormones, vanity, and greed.
           I spend my day at peddling soaps and creams
           With which a person may deceive themselves,
           Believing thereby they attain to beauty,   5
           Ne'er knowing beauty's only found within.
           It were an excellent job that were made
           In the midway 'twixt this and prophecy:
           The one's too like an image speaking false,
           The other too like children, ever tattling.   10

Enter CADY HERON *and* DAMIAN *aside, browsing.*

CADY   Good day, my friends. Take heed: in those three
                                                         women's
           Midst I have spent mine hours auxiliary.
           They write within a Burn Book, where an army
           Of slander gives them some esprit de corps.
JANIS   What doth it say of me?
CADY   —Thou'rt not within.   15
JANIS   O wenches vile, who mock their sisters so.
                                   [*Damian approaches them.*
DAMIAN   This lotion, shall it minimize my pores?
JANIS   Nay. [*To Cady:*] Caddy, thou must take the wretched

book.

CADY	Not on my life.
JANIS	—'Twould be an act of justice!
	We could the pages publish, that our school 20
	Would know how, like an ax, she woundeth all.
CADY	I do not steal, 'tis not within my nature.
JANIS	[*to Damian:*] Thou jester, thou dost browse at cream
	for feet.
	[*To Cady:*] Kind Caddy, evil calls in double voice:
	There is the evil that doth evil acts, 25
	Which is, as all do know, detestable.
	The other evil, though, is eviler—
	'Tis people who, though seeing evil acts,
	Stand meekly by, do naught to end the wrong.

Enter MADAM NORBURY, *browsing.*

DAMIAN	Mean'st thou I, then, am bound by obligation 30
	That lady's horrid garments to destroy?
	Wait, now I see—'tis Madam Norbury!
JANIS	How I do love to see a teacher when
	She is not in the schoolhouse, by my troth—
	'Tis like a dog who walketh 'pon hind legs! 35
NORBURY	Good afternoon, I did not see ye here.
JANIS	Here stand I, practicing my calling true:
	To peddle moderately valued soap.
DAMIAN	Are you here shopping, Madam Norbury?
NORBURY	Nay, hither came I with my paramour— 40
	The scruffy fellow yonder whom you see.
	'Tis but a jest—sometimes we elders joke.
DAMIAN	My nana, when inebriated, doth

	Remove her false hair from atop her pate.	
NORBURY	Thy nana and myself have this in common.	45
	The truth is, I do work a second job	
	As bartender for two nights ev'ry week,	
	O'er at P. J. Calamity's nearby.	
	Requir'd am I to wear this button'd vest	
	And, each new day, more buttons to acquire—	50
	I fetch me trifles, and return again,	
	As from a voyage, rich with merchandise.	
JANIS	[*aside:*] In faith, it seems she hath it worse than me.	
NORBURY	I hope thou shalt join Mathletes, Cady, for	
	We start our meetings in a fortnight's time.	55
	'Twould be well for the team to have a lass—	
	E'en thus the team could meet a lass for once.	
CADY	Methinks 'twould be a pleasure; I shall join.	
NORBURY	Magnificent! Thy presence shall be welcome.	
DAMIAN	'Tis social suicide to join that team.	60
NORBURY	My thanks, kind Damian. This scene hath been	
	Sufficient in its awkwardness replete.	
	Upon the morrow I shall see ye three.	
CADY	Farewell.	
NORBURY	—Farewell.	

[Exit Madam Norbury.

JANIS	—How bleak her character.	
	Back to the main: when shalt thou see Regina?	65
CADY	Make not too rash a trial of me, for	
	I'm gentle and not fearful. Still, I may	
	Not spy upon her anymore; 'tis wrong.	
JANIS	She never shall discover what thou dost—	
	'Twill be a secret shar'd among we three.	70
CADY	I'll think upon the matter further, Janis.	

[Exeunt Cady and Damian.

JANIS   Perchance withal Regina I'm obsess'd—
Pray judge not until ye are thus distress'd.

[Exit Janis.

SCENE 3

At the Heron residence and North Shore High School.

Enter CADY HERON.

CADY   How did it come to be, my very first
Friends, kindlier than any since my birth,
Have made me feel life's out of my control?
This situation is a bitter pill.

The phone rings and CADY *answers it.*
Enter REGINA GEORGE *aside, on the phone.*

REGINA   I know thy secret. Say, is it thy will   5
To make a stale of me amongst these mates?

CADY   [*aside:*] Alack! Am I so suddenly discover'd?
Shall I apologize? Begin to cry?
Nay, calm remain until thou knowest all.
[*To Regina:*] A secret? What is this of which thou
                                            speak'st?   10

REGINA   Sweet Gretchen said thou likest Aaron Samuels.
Nor care I, truly—do whate'er thou will'st.

	Let me speak honestly of Aaron's traits:	
	He careth but for mother, school, and friends.	
CADY	Yet, is this bad?	
REGINA	—If thou lik'st him, 'tis well.	15
	Wouldst thou have me speak to him, for thy sake?	
CADY	Wouldst thou be so kindhearted, e'en for me?	
	Thou shalt say naught embarrassing, I hope.	
REGINA	Nay, trust my wisdom, Cady. 'Tis a game	
	In which I ever hold the upper hand.	20
	Yet ere thou goest, tell me: art thou mad	
	That Gretchen told me of thy fondness for him?	
CADY	No, never.	
REGINA	—An thou art, pray tell me so.	
	'Twas base and baseless both for her to do.	

Enter Gretchen Wieners *above, on balcony, on the phone.*

CADY	'Twas base, indeed, and yet I hold no grudge.	25
	Belike she doth enjoy attention's spotlight.	
REGINA	Thou hearest, Gretchen? Thus I said to thee:	
	Our Cady is not angry at thine act.	
GRETCHEN	Thou thinkest I enjoy attention's spotlight?	
	The rudeness that appear'd in me have I	30
	Learned from my entertainment at thy hands.	
CADY	[*aside:*] Regina trapp'd me in a rigid vise.	
REGINA	Good even, ladies. We'll meet on the morrow.	

> [*Exeunt Regina and Gretchen.*
> *Cady walks to school.*

CADY	I have endur'd a three-way calling strike,	
	Yet also found a diamond in the rough:	35
	Regina's blessing given, I may speak	

To Aaron further, that we closer draw.

Enter AARON SAMUELS.

'Twas on October third he ask'd the date—
By calendar, not for a date, I mean.
'Twas two weeks later when we spake again.   40

AARON   The rain doth fall.

CADY   [*aside:*]   —O, observation plain.

[*To Aaron:*] Indeed it doth, with drops both wet and
                      falling.

[*Aside:*] This budding romance must progress apace,
Lest our small play extendeth many hours.
Mine instincts shall I follow—my affections   45
Are then most humble; I have no ambition
To see a goodlier man. [*To Aaron:*] Say, canst thou help?
These math equations lose me utterly.
[*Aside:*] I am not lost, yet shall be so for him.

AARON   Indeed.

CADY   [*aside:*]   —Quite clear is Madam Norbury.   50
I've no need of his help, but for my heart.

AARON   Factorial it is, so multiply
Each one by n.

CADY   [*aside:*]   —'Tis wrong. [*To Aaron:*] Is't the
                      summation?

AARON   Forsooth, they are the selfsame.

CADY   [*aside:*]   —Wrong again.
The lad's so wrong, yet so right for my love.   55
[*To Aaron:*] My thanks, 'tis clearer now that thou hast
                      help'd.

AARON   Tonight, a party for All Hallows' Eve

	Shall happen at the house of my friend Chris.	
	Wilt thou go thither?	
CADY	—Yea, with all delight.	

[Aaron hands Cady a piece of paper.

AARON	The address thou mayst find upon this sheet.	60
	It is a costume ball, and many who	
	Attend do make the most of their attire.	
CADY	I understand and shall with joy attend.	
AARON	The sheet admitteth but one person only—	
	I prithee, bring no paramour withal.	65
CADY	Grool. O! The word intended to be "cool,"	
	Yet mix'd with "great" before it pass'd my lips.	
AARON	'Tis grool, indeed. I shall see thee tonight.	

[Exit Aaron.

Enter KEVIN GNAPOOR.

KEVIN	Hail, Africa. Shalt thou attend the meeting?	
	The Mathletes shall begin our work today,	70
	And thou art critical to our equation.	
CADY	Wait thou a moment and I shall return.	

[Exit Kevin.

	'Twas lying, saying this to Kevin here.	
	Yet I must homeward to create a costume,	
	For Aaron said to make the most of it.	75
	What horrid monster shall I be tonight?	
	Mayhap a werewolf with long fangs and snout,	
	And claws to make all Baskerville afraid?	
	Perchance I shall in green conceal my face,	
	Like frightful monster made by Frankenstein?	80
	Or, peradventure, I shall be a witch,	

With warts and spells to work my classmates woe!
A-ha, I know! I'll be a zombie bride.
Such fun—I cannot wait till eventide!

[Exit Cady.

SCENE 4

At the All Hallows' Eve party.

Enter Gretchen Wieners *and* Karen Smith.

GRETCHEN   I can say little more than I have studied—
                    This question's out of my part: what art thou?
KAREN   A mouse, of course, I bid thee see mine ears!

[Exeunt Gretchen and Karen.

Enter Cady Heron.

CADY   In normal world, 'tis Halloween when the
                    Kids dress for candy's sake. By feminine
                    Rule, lasses dress with purpose and mystique.

5

Enter Regina George *and* Lady George *above, on balcony.*

LADY G.   How well thou look'st, my dear! How innocent.
REGINA   My bosom and my derrière are fine,
                    And on display to celebrate the dead!

[Exeunt Regina and Lady George.

CADY   It is the one night in the year entire   10
              When lasses are array'd most wantonly
              And other girls say nothing of the fault,
              For all declare 'tis nothing but a costume.
              The boldest lasses dress in lingerie
              And furry ears of little animals.   15
              Yet none did tell me of th'unspoken rule
              By which a lass may wear a strumpet's outfit.
              Thus, like a soul awoken from the grave,
              I have arriv'd array'd beneath death's veil.

Enter REGINA GEORGE, GRETCHEN WIENERS, KAREN SMITH, AARON
SAMUELS, SETH MOSAKOWSKI, *and many* STUDENTS *in costumes.*

              The ball begins and I am out of place.   20
              I stick out like the sorest thumb of all—
              As if a legion full of blacksmiths had
              Ta'en out collected vengeance on a thumb.
              Behold my classmates watch as women kiss,
              An 'twere a spectacle for all to see.   25
              Ah, there is Gretchen next to Karen talking—
              Familiar faces shall be welcome now.
              [*To Gretchen and Karen:*] Good even, friends!
KAREN   —Why art
                                        thou so attir'd,
              In clothes wherewith to scare the bravest person?
CADY   It is All Hallows' Eve and thus it suits.   30
GRETCHEN   Hast thou seen Jason? I expect him here.
KAREN   One lad I know is looking fine tonight:
              Seth Mosakowski.
GRETCHEN   —What, that simple fop?

KAREN   The same, indeed. He kisses by the book.

GRETCHEN   He is thy cousin.

KAREN   —Yea, but only first.   35

GRETCHEN   Indeed.

KAREN   —There are mere cousins and first cousins,
Then second cousins and so on from there.

GRETCHEN   Nay, sweet.

KAREN   —This is not how a fam'ly works?

GRETCHEN   'Tis wrong in ev'ry way.

                                   [Aaron approaches Cady.

AARON   —Thou hast arriv'd,
And bringest, too, a zombie bride withal.   40

CADY   Ex-wife to be precise.

AARON   —Original.
Wilt thou a drink, which I may bring to thee?

CADY   With pleasure.

AARON   —On the instant I'll return.

CADY   My thanks, kind Aaron.

                      [Aaron walks aside. Karen waves at Seth.

GRETCHEN   —Karen, cease at once.
Be not so taken in.

KAREN   —O Seth, I come!   45
Did ever dragon keep so fair a cave?

                            [Karen approaches Seth.
                            Regina approaches Aaron.

REGINA   Good evening.

AARON   —O, how well thou look'st tonight.
Did no one tell thee thou shouldst wear a costume?
Couldst thou not bear All Hallows' Eve t'observe?

REGINA   Asses are made to bear, and so are you.   50
Pray stop thy tongue: I have some news to share.

	Thou knowest Cady, newly come to school?
AARON	Forsooth, she seemeth sweet and passing kind.
	Upon my invitation hath she come.
REGINA	Be careful, for she has a crush on thee, 55
	Each night doth pine for thee upon her pillow,
	And sigheth, "Aaron, make me soon thy bride!"
AARON	Indeed? How cam'st thou by this knowledge rare?
REGINA	[*aside:*] My strategy doth fail, he is not mov'd,
	Except unto a greater interest! 60
	Therefore I'll dig the hole e'en deeper yet.
	[*To Aaron:*] The lass hath told me—ev'ryone, in fact.
	It is naively cute, how heartily
	She bareth all her feelings to the world.
	She hath the wisdom of a little girl, 65
	Who writeth on her notebook constantly,
	With hearts declaring "Madam Aaron Samuels."
	She fashion'd, too, a tunic with thy face,
	Which doth proclaim "My heart for Aaron e'er!"
	She wears it always underneath her garments— 70
	E'en now, I'll wager, doth she sport the tunic.
AARON	Thou art in jest.
REGINA	—Yet who could blame the lass?
	Thou e'er wert gorgeous to mine eyes, thou know'st.
	Take heed: I do not say she stalketh thee,
	Yet she did save the tissue thou didst use, 75
	An 'twere the relic of a holy saint,
	And said she would perform some Afric voodoo
	With which to turn thy heart unto her own.
	[*Cady waves at Aaron from afar.*
AARON	Can this be true? Yet there, across the way,
	A zombie bride—ex-wife—doth wave at me, 80

Portending some strange fate that may be knit.

CADY [*aside:*] E'en yonder doth Regina speak for me,
      Her words fall gently on his waiting ears,
      For see, he waveth like a lad in love.

REGINA 'Tis true the lass is socially inept   85
        And strange beyond all natural degree,
        Yet she hath been a constant friend to me.
        Thus, promise thou shalt not make sport of her.

AARON 'Tis certain I shall not make sport of her.

CADY [*aside:*] How can kind Janis hate Regina so?   90
      For look how she doth take my suit to him.
      She is so good and decent, by my troth.

                                    [*Regina kisses Aaron.*

      Alack and rue the day! Thou harlot rank!

AARON What art thou playing at, Regina? Cease!
       'Twas thou who ended our relationship.   95

REGINA Thou speakest foolishness—why would I so?
        Thou art the finest lad at North Shore High.

                              [*Regina kisses Aaron again.*
                              Exeunt all except Cady.

CADY Ne'er have I felt betrayal such as this—
      O, woe the day! My heart rings in mine ears,
      My stomach shall escape straight through my bowels. 100
      The lump that rises in my gorge is like
      A bulky pill one swallows sans a drink.
      Regina George, how I despise thee so—
      My hate for thee doth only grow and grow!

                                          [*Exit Cady.*

SCENE 5

At the Ian residence, and in the next days
and weeks at North Shore High School.

Enter JANIS IAN *and* DAMIAN, *watching a horror film.*

JANIS	A friend to watch a scary movie with,
	Whilst all around us people celebrate
	All Hallows' Eve with fear and horrid masks—
	The perfect night, as Damian and I
	Sit here as merry as the day is long.

Enter CADY HERON.

DAMIAN	Alas, the zombie from the film doth live!
CADY	Regina hath ta'en Aaron back e'en now—
	Then show'd what perfect kisses they have form'd!
JANIS	Poor Caddy!
CADY	—Wherefore would she take him back?
JANIS	The lady is a ruiner of lives—
	'Tis what she doth, a calling she doth follow.
DAMIAN	When we were but thirteen, she forc'd our class
	To sign a false petition to declare
	That our fair Janis was none other than—
JANIS	Nay, Damian! Speak not. The vixen shall
	Forbidden be to ply her villainy!
	Is she not proven in the height a villain,
	That slander'd, scorn'd, dishonor'd my kinswoman?
	We must take action.

5

10

15

CADY   —Must we?
JANIS   —Follow on.
          Regina George: an evil dictator.   20
          How doth a state o'erthrow such tyranny?
          Cut off her plentiful resources, yea.
          Regina would be naught without her men:
          Each one high status, handsome in the height,
          We shall her Aaron welcome to our side.   25
          Her body—technic'ly, a perfect thing—
          Shall soon become a liability.
          Her band of loyal, skanky followers
          Anon shall turn to fervent enemies.
          Good Caddy, if thou wouldst this future see,   30
          Thou must approach them in the guise of friendship,
          Like nothing were awry 'twixt her and thee.

	Canst thou accomplish this? Art strong enow?
CADY	I shall, to take my justified revenge.
JANIS	Let us, then, turn the hag's world upside down.

                                                 [Exeunt.

The following day. Enter CADY HERON,
in the hallway of North Shore High School.

CADY	Pretending naught is wrong shall simple be,
	For no one doth enjoy continued conflict.

Enter GRETCHEN WIENERS.

GRETCHEN	Kind Cady, it is well to find thee here.
	Regina ask'd me to convey to thee
	That she attempted to connect ye two—
	E'en Aaron and thyself—yet his sole aim
	Was with Regina to be reconcil'd.
	'Tis no fault of Regina's, thou canst see.
CADY	Of course not, nay.
GRETCHEN	—Thou, then, dost hold no grudge?
CADY	By heaven, no.
GRETCHEN	—Hurrah for friendship's glow!
	Regina ask'd me to deliver this.

                           [Gretchen embraces Cady. Exit Gretchen.

Enter REGINA GEORGE, *sipping a drink, and* AARON SAMUELS, *aside.*

REGINA	My weight shall be improvèd by this plan:
	The South Beach Fat Flush, wherein I shall drink
	The juice of cranberries for three whole days.

AARON	Thou drinkest not the juice of cranberries: 50
	'Tis cocktail cranberry, near wholly sugar.
REGINA	But three pounds more to lose, and I may rest.
AARON	Thou art absurd.

[Regina sees Cady.

REGINA	[*to Aaron:*] —Thy hair, why is it so?
	Yet push it back and thou, like Samson, shall
	Have hair to tempt Delilahs ev'rywhere. 55
	Ah, Cady, canst thou tell sweet Aaron dear
	His hair is sexier when 'tis push'd back?
CADY	[*aside:*] O, how she dangleth him before mine eyes,
	As if he were a morsel, I a dog.
	If 'twere the world of animals I knew, 60
	I'd jump at her and knock her from her seat,
	Whilst baring claws and teeth to work her woe.
	The other animals would then surround
	Us, yelling fervently as we did rage.
	How do I long to bring such anger forth, 65
	Yet cannot, for the sake of decency—
	'Tis Girl World, not the world of animals;
	In Girl World every fight must be conceal'd.
	[*To Aaron:*] Thy hair doth sexy look when 'tis push'd
	back.
AARON	Betwixt these two, a lad could be too lov'd. 70

[Exit Aaron.

REGINA	The juice of cranberries my skin doth blemish!
CADY	I have a skin cream that may help thy plight.
	[*Aside:*] I have secur'd foot cream from Janis' shop,
	To give it to Regina for her face.
	Whenever opportunity ariseth, 75
	We shall ply sabotage to make her squirm.

       [Cady hands Regina the foot cream.
[*To Regina:*] This is for thee, to help thy visage glow.

       Enter AARON SAMUELS.

AARON   I have return'd to thee again, small chuck.
                   [He kisses Regina on the cheek.
      Thy face doth smell of sweetest peppermint!
CADY   [*aside:*] Alas, 'twas not the scent I did intend!   80
            [Exeunt Regina and Aaron together.
                 Exit Cady severally.

       Enter JANIS IAN.

JANIS   Impeccable revenge must tailor'd be
      Unto the villain who hath done the wrong,
      And thus I've taken liberties with scissors,

Amending horrible Regina's tunic—
Two holes I've open'd where her breasts would go,   85
To make her foolish to the multitudes.

[Janis hides.

Enter REGINA GEORGE *with holes in her tunic.*

REGINA   Though this is not the fashion, I shall wear't,
Head lifted high, for all the world to see.
Whilst confidently I do strut the halls,
Whoever plied this silly trick on me   90
Shall find themselves upset by their own trick.
And I, the meanwhile, shall not rest nor sleep,
Till I can find occasion of revenge.

Enter other FEMALE STUDENTS, *including* LEA EDWARDS, *dressed
similarly with holes in their clothes. Some students sell candy canes.*

JANIS   [*aside:*] What universe illogical is this?
Hath vile Regina so convinc'd the minds   95
Of these, my fellow students, that they follow
Her ev'ry movement an 'twere holy writ?
Is there no sense remaining at this school?
This shall not stop my pains, but urge them on:
Is't possible disdain should die while she   100
Hath such meet food to feed it as Regina?

[Exit Regina.

Enter CADY HERON *and* DAMIAN, *aside.*

A month entire our efforts we have plied,

	With little of success, except that we
	Did make Regina's face smell like a foot.
DAMIAN	My time hath all been spent in choral practice. 105
JANIS	Belike our current aim is misapplied—
	We'll turn to Gretchen Wieners, make her crack,
	Attack Regina from her closest flank.
	If we can crack the lock that Gretchen holds,
	We'll find the key unto Regina's past, 110
	Which, opening, shall soon reveal a pit
	Of filth and muck.
DAMIAN	—Speak "crack" once more.
JANIS	—Crack,
	crack!
	We'll reconvene this evening.
CADY	—I cannot.
	Regina doth expect me at rehearsal—
	The talent show is drawing ever nearer. 115
	We're dancing to a song—
BOTH	—'Tis "Jingle Bell Rock."
CADY	Ye both the song know? What coincidence!
JANIS	All in the English-speaking world do know't.
DAMIAN	'Tis, ev'ry year, the dance they do perform,
	Like clockwork programm'd by the yuletide moon. 120
CADY	This year, 'tis mine to learn. Behold, my friends—
	Regina hither comes, pray get ye gone.

[Exeunt Janis and Damian.

Enter REGINA GEORGE.

| REGINA | Didst thou just converse with Janis Ian? |
| CADY | Surprising 'twas to me as well, for she |

Is strange past speaking. By my modesty,   125
The jewel in my dow'r, I would not wish
Any companion in the world but thee.
She did approach and spake to me of crack!

REGINA The word "pathetic" was design'd for her.
Of Janis Ian I shall tell thee this: 130
In middle school we two were best of friends—
'Tis shocking, yea? Embarrassing as well!
Yet in eighth grade, I found a paramour—
A lad most fair, my first in love's embrace,
His name was Kyle, who mov'd to Indiana.   135
The point is that odd Janis turn'd a shade
Of green that mark'd her jealousy of him.
If e'er I did refuse to meet with her
When I would rather spend my time with Kyle,
She angrily stood 'fore me to demand,   140
"Say wherefore thou didst not return my call!"
I would rejoinder, "Wherefore art thou so?
Why so obsess'd by how I spend my time?"
When next my birthday party did arrive,
A party just for lasses, by the pool,   145
I told her, "Janis, thou art not invited.
It seems thine appetite doth turn to ladies—
To put it plain: thou art a lesbian."
No lesbian could to my party come,
Not with so many lasses clad in swimwear!   150
How she would ogle them with shameless eyes!
Her mother call'd my mother to complain,
Full yelling at her—'twas beyond the pale.
Then Janis, sadly, left the school, for ne'er
Would any lass speak further unto her.   155

         When she return'd to high school in the fall,
         Her hair was chopp'd and strange had she become—
         Too like a witch, and with the spells to match.
         By thine account, she now hath ta'en to crack.
         [*To Lea:*] By all that is divine, thy lovely skirt—   160
         A stunning, fashionable garment 'tis!
         How didst thou come by such a lovely thing?

CADY   [*aside:*] Regina's words, they echo in mine ears!
         She once with these same words did praise my bracelet.

LEA   'Twas once my mother's, in the nineteen eighties.   165

REGINA   A vintage piece—adorable it is!

                                    [*Exit Lea.*

         [*To Cady:*] The skirt is uglier than hell's own heart.

CADY   [*aside:*] A two-fac'd lady, wicked through and through.
         [*To Regina:*] Shalt thou send candy canes unto thy

                                    friends?

REGINA   I do not send them, nay, I just receive.   170
         Thou must send me one, too, thou silly wench.
         Take care until I see thee next, sweet friend.

                                 [*Exit Regina.*

CADY   O, I shall send her canes, with limps to match.
         Three candy canes shall crack one Gretchen Wieners.

            [*Cady approaches the candy cane sellers.*

         I prithee, three delicious candy canes,   175
         Wherewith I may spread joy, good will, and cheer.

             [*Cady enters English class and sits with other
                    students. Exeunt some students.*

Enter ENGLISH TEACHER, GRETCHEN WIENERS, *and other* STUDENTS.

ENGLISH   We shall begin today with Julius Caesar:

"Why, man, he doth bestride the narrow world
Like a Colossus"—this doth translate to,
"Why is he passing vain and so obnoxious?"   180

Enter DAMIAN, *dressed like Santa Claus.*

DAMIAN	Ho ho ho! Candygrams for all and each!
ENGLISH	Be swift, I bid thee, learning is afoot.
DAMIAN	Behold, I've two for Taylor Zimmerman.
	Glenn Cocco, four for thee! Thou art well lik'd!
	And Caddy Heron, is she in this class? 185
CADY	'Tis Cady.
DAMIAN	—Cady, one for thee have I,
	And none for Gretchen Wieners, verily.
GRETCHEN	Methought I should receive one if thou didst—

	Who is it from?	

CADY   [*reading:*]   —"Mine utmost thanks that thou
Art such a dear friend unto me. Regina."   190
'Tis sweet of her to think of me so kindly.

ENGLISH   Now back to Caesar and his fall from grace.

CADY   [*aside:*] I'll warrant, now that Gretchen doth believe
Regina's ire is focus'd onto her,
The secrets shall pour forth as water from   195
An ocean fill'd with tears. Now must I wait:
The board is set, the pieces are arrang'd,
And Gretchen is the knight unto my queen.
The perfect secret shall she share anon,
And when she doth, Regina is my pawn.   200

                                          [Exeunt.

ACT
III

SCENE 1

The North Shore High School talent show.

Enter STUDENTS *as audience, including* JASON
in the front row and AARON SAMUELS. *Enter* PARENTS *as*
audience also, including SIR HERON, LADY HERON,
and LADY GEORGE. *Enter* SIR DUVALL *on the stage.*

DUVALL   Good evening, friends. You are most welcome to
The North Shore High School winter talent show!
Will ye break forth in thunderous applause,
That our performers, who do wait offstage,
May know you bring your uttermost support?   5
                  [The audience applauds and cheers.
Cease now, ere senseless rioting erupts.
Our first act for our wondrous talent show
Doth call himself a star of rising height.
I prithee, clap your hands for Damian.

Enter DAMIAN *on the stage.*

DAMIAN   [*sings:*] Each day with thee is wonderful,   10
        Each hour joy springs anew,
        Each moment feeleth bountiful
          When thou dost love me, too.

Enter CADY HERON, GRETCHEN WIENERS,
and KAREN SMITH *above, on balcony, preparing for their act.*

GRETCHEN   O, wherefore would Regina send her canes
                     To ye two lasses, but not me as well?   15
KAREN   Perchance she hath forgotten thou exist'st.
CADY   Her acts of late no court would legalize—
                     It seems to some great oddness she gives birth.
                     Is something, mayhap, out of her control?
GRETCHEN   She told me, recently, her parents two   20
                     No longer share a bed in their own house—
                     Perchance 'tis such as this that thou dost mean.
                     By Jove, I bid thee tell her not my words,
                     For like a squirrel trapp'd within a box
                     They fled my mouth as quick as legs could run.   25
JASON   [to Damian:] Thou art a fop—I bite my thumb at thee!
DAMIAN   [sings:] My beauty's inexpressible,
                          No word shall bring me down.
                     Were thy love inaccessible,
                          'Twould shame my kingly crown.   30
                                    [The audience claps. Exit Damian.
GRETCHEN   Good Cady, no offense to thee I aim,
                     Yet wherefore would she send thee candy canes?
                     She doth not even like thee much. Alas—
                     I call in question the continuance
                     Of her great love. Mayhap she feeleth weird   35
                     While in my presence, for 'tis only I
                     Who knows the truth of how she chang'd her nose
                     By prowess of physician talented.
                     Once more these words rush forth, escape my lips,
                     Like chickens running from the butcher's block.   40
                                    [Exeunt Cady, Gretchen, and Karen.

Enter KEVIN GNAPOOR and his FRIENDS on stage as the next act.

KEVIN   [*reciting:*] Unlock thine ear, each horrible MC—
                    There's naught at which thou greater art than me,
               From grades I earn to my keen poetry,
                    No one may lay a hand on Kevin G.
               A Mathlete I, so yea, nerd is inferr'd,   45
                    Yet still thou must forget all thou hast heard—
               Forsooth, I am like Sir James Bond the Third,
                    This Kevin likes it shaken—never stirr'd.
               The G is mute when I sneak in thy door,
                    And satisfy thy wench upon the floor,   50
               Thou shalt be sure 'tis I she doth adore
                    When she doth cry, "More, more, Kevin Gnapoor!"

DUVALL   My thanks, good Kevin—now thine act is o'er.
               Thou hast our ears assaulted long enow.

KEVIN   A happy holiday to ev'ryone.   55
               We hope ye did enjoy our number—ha!

                                        [*The audience claps.*
                                  Exeunt Kevin and his friends.

DUVALL   This act was K. G. and the pow'r of three.
               It may be said: 'twas something to behold.

Enter CADY HERON, REGINA GEORGE, GRETCHEN WIENERS,
and KAREN SMITH *on the stage, lining up in preparation for their act.*
Enter JANIS IAN *and* DAMIAN *above, on balcony, watching.*

DAMIAN   Doth it bring any anger to thy soul,
               That still they use thy choreography?   60

JANIS   Nay, stop at once—I am not bother'd by't;
               My heart keeps on the windy side of care.

Enter KEVIN GNAPOOR *behind them, on balcony.*

KEVIN	As I do breathe, thou art a lovely lass,
	And prime among the others at our school.
JANIS	Why starest thou?
KEVIN	—I happily would see 65
	Thee on the stage instead of these four lasses,
	To sway and swing and swerve with symmetry.

[Exit Kevin.

DAMIAN	A passing forward fellow, by my troth!

[Exeunt Janis and Damian.

REGINA	Before our act beginneth, Gretchen, hear:
	Thou must switch sides with Cady in a trice. 70
GRETCHEN	Yet I am wont to stand upon thy left,
	And ever have been lo these many years.
REGINA	When we were three, then such was sensible,
	Yet now, as four, the tallest take the center.
GRETCHEN	The dance entire shall backward be to me. 75
	See? I am wont to stand upon thy left!
REGINA	Thou show'st a tender sisterly regard,
	To wish me dance with one half lunatic;
	At present, thou art on my final nerve.
	I shall not say't again: switch thou anon. 80

[Cady and Gretchen exchange places.

DUVALL	Our final act! Pray, welcome to the stage
	The helpers of rever'd Saint Nicholas
	With their song: "Rousing Rock to Jingle Bell."

[A recorded singer begins playing as Cady,
Regina, Gretchen, and Karen begin dancing.

RECORD	[*sings:*] When jingle bells begin to ring,
	Their jolly tune, their jolly swing, 85
	Then angel bands in concert sing,
	Hey nonny, nonny, ho ho ho!

The snow a'blowing—O, such fun,
　　The jingle hopping hath begun,
Make merry yuletide, ev'ryone—   90
　　Hey nonny, nonny, ho ho ho!
　　　　　[Gretchen becomes confused and bumps into
　　　　　Regina. Gretchen trips on the recording device,
　　　　　　　　　　　which malfunctions.

RECORD   [*sings:*] O jin—O jin—O jin—O jin—O jin—

REGINA   [*aside to Gretchen:*] Fix it, and quickly too, ere we are
　　　　　　　　　　　　　　　　sham'd!
　　　　　[Gretchen kicks the recording device,
　　　　　sending it into the air. It strikes Jason
　　　　　in the face, and the music stops.

GRETCHEN   My Jason, O my sweet—apologies!

CADY   [*sings:*] A time so bright, a perfect night,   95
　　　　　A rousing rock shall do us right,
　　　　　The jingle bells bring us the light,
　　　　　　Hey nonny, nonny, ho ho ho!
　　　　　　　　　[All join in singing the song.
　　　　　O jingle horse, lift up thy feet,
　　　　　A happy company to meet,   100
　　　　　Our feet enjoy a merry beat,
　　　　　　Hey nonny, nonny, ho ho ho!
　　　　　　　[The audience claps and cheers. Exeunt students
　　　　　　　and parents in audience. Exit Sir Duvall.

KAREN   'Twas better than it ever went before!

　　　　　　Enter AARON SAMUELS.

AARON   Well done, sweet lasses, wondrous in th'extreme!
　　　　　　　　　[Aaron begins to kiss Regina.

REGINA   Nay, Aaron.

AARON   —What, art thou asham'd of me?   105

REGINA   No, sir, God forbid; but asham'd to kiss,
Because in doing thou shalt smear my gloss.

Enter KEVIN GNAPOOR, *passing through.*

KEVIN   Well dancèd, Africa. 'Twas perfect, by
My calculation.

CADY   —Many thanks, indeed!

                                     [Exit Kevin.

GRETCHEN   Look how the lass doth blush with cheeks of red—   110
            Thou likest him, or I do nothing know.
CADY   Nay, 'tis not true.
GRETCHEN   —'Tis wherefore thou wouldst be
            A Mathlete, to be closer to thy love.
AARON   The Mathletes? Thou? Thou hatest mathematics.
GRETCHEN   Behold, her cheeks are redder than her tunic.   115
            Thou lovest him and he thinks well of thee.
            'Tis fetch!
REGINA   —Nay, Gretchen, "fetch" shall never catch,
            Stop hosting an event no one attends.
            It shall not hap—the zeitgeist thou art not.
            The fad is bad; I'm mad and thou art sad.   120

                            [Exeunt Regina, Karen,
                                and Aaron.

GRETCHEN   O, when I am again in English class,
            I know what is th'report that I shall make:
            We study Caesar and his mighty acts;
            I'll lay him low. For who is Caesar, eh?
            And wherefore should great Caesar be allow'd   125
            To stomp and lumber like a giant brute
            Whilst we do hide from his enormous feet,
            Attempting, fearfully, to stay unscath'd?
            Whence cometh all the honors he hath earn'd?
            Consider Brutus—is he not as fine,   130
            As smart, as likeable as Caesar, too?
            When did it happen that a single person
            Became the boss of ev'ryone around?
            'Tis not what our proud Rome doth stand for, nay!
            We should, therefore, stab Caesar—stab and stab—   135
            And let his blood flow down in righteous streams!

CADY   [*aside:*] 'Tis plain that Gretchen Wieners hath been
                                                    crack'd.

GRETCHEN   O, Cady, if thou only knew'st how vile,
            How reprehensible, how knavish, and
            How horrible Regina truly is!   140
            Thou knowest I may not hoop earrings wear?
            'Twas two full years ago she did declare
            Hoop earrings as her purview only, yea—
            The bound'ry circular of her domain—
            Ne'ermore would I be sanction'd in the wearing.   145
            When I, for Hanukkah, receiv'd a pair
            From my dear parents—white gold hoops were they,
            Expensive in the buying, priceless in
            The giving generous—yet 'twas my lot
            To act as though I could not stand the things.   150
            She took the ring of me: I'll none of it,
            But must contest her wickedness anon.
            Know'st thou she cheateth frequently on Aaron,
            Doth make him cuckold for another's lust?
            Each Thursday, when he thinks she is engag'd   155
            In preparation for the SAT,
            She earns him horns by being horny with
            Shane Oman, o'er in the projection room,
            Which sits above the auditorium.
            Ne'er have I shar'd this secret with a soul   160
            Because I am, I grant, a perfect friend.
            Yet knowledge of it nearly makes me burst,
            For Aaron is, in sooth, an innocent man—
            If there's a chance of resurrecting love,
            I'm not above returning to the start,   165
            To find out where the heartache did begin.

CADY   O, Gretchen, thou hast put thy trust in me;
              In faith, I'll prove a better friend than she.

                                                          [Exeunt.

SCENE 2

At North Shore High School.

Enter JANIS IAN.

JANIS   The confidence that Gretchen puts in Caddy,
              Hath giv'n us power to fulfill our plan:
              The weapon loaded, ready to engage,
              She is the mark, we executioners,
              Prepar'd, with words, to end her villainy.   5
              I'll make a voyage with her to the devil,
              And, when we meet him, she shall see herself.
              Now Christmas break hath pass'd, our plan is set:
              Each Thursday Caddy, Damian, and I
              Shall help young Aaron see Regina's deeds—   10
              Red-handed in Shane Oman's greedy arms.
              I'll warrant the projection room shall show
              Far more than its original intent.

                                                          [Exit Janis.

Enter AARON SAMUELS, *reading a leaflet.*
Enter REGINA GEORGE *and* SHANE OMAN *aside,*
in projection room, kissing in their undergarments.

AARON　　　This puzzling notice maketh little sense,

Confounding is the message thereupon:　　　15

"The practice for the swim team shall be held

In the projection room, which is above

The auditorium." Is this not strange?

Is there an unus'd pool conceal'd therein?

Methought the room was us'd for film, not flippers.　　　20

Yet hither have I come, though it may be

A small cocoon to practice butterfly.

　　　　　[Aaron tries to open the door, but it is jammed.

REGINA　　　Alas, who cometh to disturb our hive?

We both must hide at once, or be found out!

SHANE　　　Come, come, you wasp; in'faith, thou art too scar'd.　　　25

REGINA　　　If I be waspish, best beware my sting.

　　　　　　　　　[Regina shoves Shane aside.

　　　　　　Exit Regina. Aaron finally opens the door and

　　　　　　　　　　enters the projection room.

AARON　　　An unexpected sight is this, good Shane—

Thine undergarments are too much expos'd.

Mine eyes did look for water, it is true,

Yet hop'd I for a pool, not for a hose.　　　30

　　　　　　　　　　　[Exit Aaron.

SHANE　　　O, reputation, reputation, fie!

Yea, I have lost my reputation here!

I've lost th'immortal portion of myself,

And what remains is bestial, verily.

Farewell now, Shane: forever art thou Shame.　　　35

　　　　　　　　　　　[Exit Shane.

Enter CADY HERON.

CADY   He'll catch her yet; the scene shall have a title:
                "How Aaron caught Regina on cloud nine."

                        Enter AARON SAMUELS.

AARON   Good afternoon.
CADY   —And thee as well, kind Aaron.

Enter DAMIAN, *disguised, running past and grabbing* CADY's *handbag.*

                My satchel! Stop, thou beetle-headed thief!
                                        [Damian runs aside.
AARON   I'll capture him who did this wrong to thee.   40
CADY   It seems the vicious rogue doth head to the
                Projection room o'er th'auditorium!
                        [Aaron runs in pursuit of Damian.
                        They enter the projection room.

Enter COACH CARR *and* TRANG PAK *in projection room, kissing.*

AARON   Coach Carr? Is't you?
DAMIAN   —Trang Pak, your paramour?
                Methinks our Principal Duvall would find this odd.
                                [Exeunt Coach Carr and
                                Trang severally, in dismay.
AARON   [*aside:*] This is the second time this hapless room   45
                Hath lur'd me to a scene uncomfortable.
                I must avoid this chamber, come what may.
                        [Exit Aaron. Damian walks from
                        the room and rejoins Cady.

Enter JANIS IAN.

CADY	Companions, wherefore did we three conceive
	We could Regina trap with seeming ease?
	In matters of deceit, we're amateurs.
	O, fie upon it! Never till this day
	Have I been touch'd with anger so distemper'd.
JANIS	Nay, though we fail, we merely must regroup:
	We yet must think outside the confines of
	This tiny box wherein our minds are trapp'd.

50

55

      [Damian looks in Cady's satchel.

DAMIAN	Within thy satchel, what are Kälteen bars?
CADY	Nutrition bars that come from Sweden's shores,
	With which my caring mother often help'd
	The Afric children to increase their weight.
JANIS	Unwittingly thou hast the perfect plan!
	Pray, give these to Regina, for the bars

60

Will hang upon her waist like a disease—
If she hath caught the Caddy, then it will
Cost her a thousand pound ere she be cur'd.
Behold, she cometh with her horrid friends,   65
Go, Caddy and Kälteen, complete thy work!
          [Damian hands the bars and satchel to Cady.
                    Exeunt Janis and Damian.

Enter REGINA GEORGE, GRETCHEN WIENERS,
          and KAREN SMITH.

CADY   Regina! She to whom I long'd to speak.
              I know thou hast attempted to lose weight,
              And I may have the answer thou dost seek.

REGINA   Indeed? Say on.

CADY   —These are nutrition bars.   70
              My mother useth them to shed her weight.
              Mayhap they can assist thee in thy quest?

REGINA   I prithee, let me have one from thee quickly!
                    [Regina takes a bar and begins eating it.
              The language on the package—is it Swedish?
              Not since IKEA have I seen such words.   75

CADY   They come from Sweden, where the girls are thin.
              Unique ingredients are found therein,
              Which are not legal in our country yet.

REGINA   Ephedrine?

CADY   —Nay.

REGINA   —Then phentermine.

CADY   —Nay, nay.
              Another element that burneth carbs: 80
              Thy carbohydrates gone within a flash,

	A pyre of health within thy stomach flat,	
	Which leadeth unto thinness in a trice.	
REGINA	Most happily I'd lose a quarter stone.	
	[*Aside:*] Why do they not object? Think they 'tis true?	85
GRETCHEN	Nay, by the heavens, what is this thou sayest?	
KAREN	Thou art already thin, Regina.	
REGINA	—Tut!	

Let us amuse ourselves in other sport:
Make over Cady with a beauty session.

> *[They begin primping and preening Cady.*

CADY   [*aside:*] 'Tis strange, when I am in Regina's presence,   90
Dislike of her doth grow each passing day,
And yet I seek to rise in her esteem.

REGINA   Thine eyebrows are two wisps of Helen's own—
Thy brow alone could launch a thousand ships.
Thou, Gretchen, step aside and let me work.   95

CADY   [*aside:*] I see the feelings swell in Gretchen, too—
How she doth long to have Regina's favor.
Each moment that Regina's specter groweth,
Poor Gretchen tries the harder to impress.
She knows 'tis better in the Plastics' sphere—   100
E'en when she hateth ev'ry passing moment—
Than to be on the outside, looking in.
Whate'er our petty arguments and fights,
To be among the Plastics bringeth fame.
We are forever in the public view,   105
And ev'ryone doth gaze with expert eyes
As if they know our secrets thoroughly.

Enter Student 8, Bethany Byrd, Jason,
and Sir Duvall *above, on balcony.*

STUD. 8	The new lass, she is come from Africa!
BETHANY	I witness'd Cady wearing pantaloons
	That cameth from some hearty army troop, 110
	And sandals of the flip-flop fashion. Yea,
	I purchas'd army pants and flip-flops, too!
JASON	The lass nam'd Cady is most beautiful,
	Belike e'en more so than Regina George.
DUVALL	'Tis whisper'd broadly that Regina George 115
	Steps out with Aaron Samuels once again.
	Canoodling, it seems, hath happen'd at
	Chris Eisel's party on All Hallows' Eve.
	Insep'rable they have been, ever since,
	An 'twere a Jack and Jill, our school the hill. 120

[*Exeunt Student 8, Bethany, Jason, and Sir*
Duvall. Exeunt Regina, Gretchen, and Karen.

CADY	A lass possess'd: e'en such have I become.
	The other day, as we did walk the halls,
	I saw Regina giving Aaron eyes,
	The two caressing cheeks and trading kisses.
	So jealous was I, watching them flirt so, 125
	I paid no mind where I was wandering
	And fell, headlong, into a refuse bin.
	O, envy that doth lead to scorn and shame—
	At least four-fifths of ev'ry hour is spent
	Discussing vile Regina with my friends, 130
	And one-fifth spent in hoping someone else
	Shall raise the topic of the heartless wench,
	That I may talk about her even more
	Sans seeming so entirely mad and foolish.

Enter JANIS IAN.

	Ah, Janis! She hath taken to my bars,	135
	Yet still I fear our plan moves sluggishly.	
	When thou dost think upon her, it is plain	
	She's not as fair as ev'ryone believes.	
JANIS	As she grows large, her breasts are magnified,	
	Vast milk jugs that could quench a legion's thirst.	140
CADY	[*aside:*] 'Tis certain ev'ryone is bor'd of me,	
	And mine incessant griping over her.	
	Yet how can I my feelings swiftly cease?	
	The words pour forth, sans remedy, from me,	
	Like vomit from the mouth of one with plague.	145
	[*To Janis:*] My theory 'tis, that if thou cutt'st her hair,	
	She would be twin unto a British man.	
JANIS	Thus have I heard, for thou said'st so before.	
	Thy jabs thou dost repeat most steadily,	
	Much like an uninvited guest who knocks	150
	Upon the clos'd door of a private banquet.	
	Instead, why not come where thou art invited?	
	Soon I shall have a showing of mine art—	
	Wilt thou take time from this, thy double life,	
	And give me thy support? I'd have thee there.	155
CADY	'Tis well.	
JANIS	—What is that smell that strikes my nose?	
CADY	Regina gifted me some fine perfume.	
JANIS	Thou smellest like a baby prostitute,	
	Preparing for a night of many trysts.	
CADY	My thanks—and now, farewell until the next.	160

[Exit Cady.

JANIS	The lass is chang'd, I fear, beyond repair.
	When first she did arrive, I welcom'd her
	As if she were a long-lost sister come—

A newfound, needed friend for Janis Ian.
Then did my perfect pair, with Damian,   165
Become a threefold miracle with her—
The complement ideal unto us both.
Alas, she did not heed my warnings dire:
With Plastic life she hath become obsess'd,
So torn by her desire for pure revenge   170
And her most earnest yearning to fit in,
She cannot choose, as one who sits upon
A fence and will not jump to either side.
She makes me sad—not mark'd or not laugh'd at,
Strikes me into a melancholy, aye.   175
O Cady, I would have my friend return—
This court of Plastics must, in time, adjourn.

                                        [Exit Janis.

SCENE 3

At North Shore High School.

Enter CADY HERON, AARON SAMUELS, KEVIN GNAPOOR,
and MADAM NORBURY, *in mathematics class.*

CADY   [*aside:*] If I would grow to be Regina's equal,
              I must talk more with Aaron. [*To Aaron:*] By all rights,
              My brain, for math, doth need a vast amendment.

AARON   Thou understandest not?

CADY   —Nay, canst thou help?
                                [Madam Norbury hands a recent
                                        examination to Cady.

NORBURY   Well done, shrewd Cady. Truly thou hast come   5
              To give my class joy and prosperity.

AARON   Thy test is nearly perfect, Cady, look—
              It seems thou understandest well enow.

CADY   [*aside:*] If I will ply this ruse upon the lad,
              I must commit entirely to my cause.   10
                                [Madam Norbury hands
                                another examination to Cady.

NORBURY   This was, however, far more disappointing.

KEVIN   Zounds, Africa, how quickly hast thou fallen,
              Like thou art antelope and math the lions.
              How went thou negative so suddenly?

AARON   How didst thou fare this time?

CADY   —Far from my goals.   15
              [*Aside:*] Yet closer to my goal another way.
              [*To Aaron:*] Methinks a tutor's skill would serve me well,

	A person who could help me understand	
	The perfect combination of two souls—	
	Er, numbers, plainly I did mean to say.	20
AARON	Most gladly would I tutor thee, if thou	
	Dost wish to have some discourse after class.	
CADY	What dost thou think Regina shall bethink?	
AARON	How could she, when you two are such close friends?	
	Or, peradventure, we shall keep it hidden.	25
	A secret's only secret when 'tis shar'd.	

> [*The bell rings. Exeunt Madam Norbury,*
> *Kevin, and all students except Cady and Aaron.*
> *They sit next to each other.*

CADY	Let us begin e'en now. This problem here—	
	How didst thou solve it? It confuseth me.	
AARON	When first I did discover its solution,	
	'Twas plain to me the answer's zero.	
CADY	[*aside:*] —Wrong.	30
	How can he be so terrible at math?	
	'Tis like a ghoul that haunts him day and night.	
	If the ill spirit have so fair a house,	
	Good things will strive to dwell with it, I'll warrant.	
AARON	When I did check my calculation, though,	35
	More clearly did the answer come: 'tis one.	
CADY	[*aside:*] A-ha! He did it, with sufficient time.	
	[*To Aaron:*] Hurrah! My answer came to one as well.	
	And, by the by, our one plus one make two.	
AARON	Perforce an answer must be deftly check'd,	40
	For often may it happen that the product	
	Of integers, which both are negative,	
	Becometh positive when multiplied.	
CADY	Like negative of four and six combin'd,	

| | Which turneth positive, to twenty-four. | 45 |

AARON   'Tis right, thou hast it right. I knew thou couldst.

CADY   Thou tutorest with skill and patience both.

                                              [They kiss.

AARON   Though this feels wondrous, 'tis not kind of us.
          We must not do it, for Regina's sake—
          'Tis most dishonest, to betray her thus.   50

CADY   Why dost thou like her? What excuse canst make?

AARON   The lady's often callous, verily—

CADY   Then wherefore dost thou like her?

AARON   —Why dost thou?
          Ask me not wherefore she is friend to me,
          When thou alike dost nearly to her bow.   55

CADY   I do not—

AARON   —Good and evil dwell inside
          The multitudes, not just Regina George.
          She is more frank, her nature doth not hide.

CADY   [*aside:*] I cannot stop the rising in my gorge—
          The vomit of my words he shall incur!   60
          [*To Aaron:*] She cheateth on thee, Aaron! Canst thou
                                                      see?
          The habit is quotidian for her.

AARON   What? Pray, depart, I'd no more speak with thee.

                                              [Exit Cady.

          Can this be true? Regina turn'd unfaithful?
          Yet even as I ask I know 'tis true,   65
          For certainly Regina is a turncoat
          Who speaketh falsely unto all she meets.
          And Cady's honest as the sun is gold,
          And shineth like that heav'nly body, too.
          She likely speaks the truth, though spitefully   70

The sentence from her baffl'd mouth escap'd.
Shall I ignore these truthful words of hers
Because she spake them with a jealous heart?
Nay, Aaron—thou art to destin'd to accept
That thy Regina hath hurt thee again.   75
Break my heart once, then all the shame's on thee—
Break my heart twice, the shame doth fall on me.

                          [Exit Aaron.

SCENE 4

*At the George residence, North Shore High School,
and clothing store.*

Enter REGINA GEORGE, *crying, with* CADY HERON,
GRETCHEN WIENERS, *and* KAREN SMITH.

KAREN   Did Aaron tell thee wherefore he decided
              That thou and he no longer should be one?
REGINA   Somebody told him of Shane Oman.
GRETCHEN   —Who?
              [*Aside:*] Doth she suspect me, since I knew the truth?
REGINA   He said 'twas someone on the baseball team—   5
              Those scoundrels who do hope to round the bases
              And dream incessantly of their next score.
              I gave him ev'rything I had, in sooth—
              Half virginal I was when first we met.
KAREN   No more of sadness and these gloomy thoughts!   10

	Let us make merry and create some sport—	
	Belike a trip to Taco Bell would suit?	
REGINA	Art mad? I cannot go to Taco Bell,	
	Not on this carbohydrate-heavy diet!	
	Thou art so foolish, Karen, by my troth!	15

[Regina begins to leave.

GRETCHEN	Regina, wait. I prithee, speak to me!
REGINA	No one doth understand my spirit's plight.
GRETCHEN	I do, and shall assist to make it right!

[Exeunt Regina and Gretchen.

CADY	Thou art not foolish, Karen. 'Tis but our	
	Concern—though she insult our minds and bodies—	20
	As her dear comrades not to shield ourselves.	
KAREN	Nay, I am foolish. Foolish is most apt—	
	There is no end, no limit, measure, bound,	
	In that word's truth; no words can that depth sound.	
	I am on course to fail most ev'ry class.	25
CADY	There's no one who doth fail at ev'rything;	
	There must be aught at which thou expert art.	
KAREN	My fist entire doth fit within my mouth,	
	An 'twere circumf'rence of the world entire.	
	Wouldst thou bear witness to the awesome feat?	30

[Karen begins putting her fist in her mouth.

CADY	Nay, I am well, though ne'er I see the sight.	
	What other skills and talents canst thou boast?	
KAREN	An thou can keep the confidence, hear on:	
	I am most nearly psychic, Cady, yea—	
	A fifth sense I possess.	
CADY	—What dost thou mean?	35
KAREN	'Tis almost like I have ESPN.	
	My breasts are like a twin prognosticatrix—	

	Protruding like a pair of weather vanes—

Protruding like a pair of weather vanes—
And can predict when clouds shall form above
To drop sweet rain upon the earth below.   40

CADY   Indeed? 'Tis most amazing, Karen, truly.

KAREN   Perchance I should say, more precisely, this:
           They recognize when it is raining.

CADY   —O.
           I know not what to say, in light of this
           Most flabbergasting power that thou hast.   45

KAREN   Another time, I may yet show it thee.

                                        [Exit Karen.

CADY   It must admitted be, I have been sad—
           Nay, utterly and greatly horrified—
           That Aaron hath not yet ask'd me to be
           His paramour, though he doth know the truth   50
           About Regina's rank, unjust deceit.
           He must be sad, of this I have no doubt,
           Yet wherefore should he mourn for her so long?
           Regina, ye will see, hath mov'd along.

                                        [Exit Cady.

Enter REGINA GEORGE *and* SHAME OMAN *above, on balcony, kissing.*
Enter LADY GEORGE *on balcony, aside.*

LADY G.   Have ye two need of aught I can provide?   55
           Mayhap a snack to strengthen weary lips?
           Perhaps a condom to prevent an heir?
           Speak up if I may offer some assistance.
           [*Aside:*] O, how they call to mind my younger self—
           Carefree and innocent as wholesome lambs.   60

                        [*Exeunt Regina, Shane, and Lady George.*

Enter CADY HERON.

CADY   Regardless, what we plan proceeds apace.
      Sweet Aaron hath dismiss'd Regina George
      And, unsuspectingly, she doth ingest
      Five thousand calories each passing day.
      Attention, now, must turn unto her horde—   65
      The army she commandeth, form'd of skanks.

Enter TEACHER *above, on balcony. Enter* JANIS IAN,
DAMIAN, REGINA GEORGE, GRETCHEN WIENERS,
and other STUDENTS, *joining* CADY *in class.*

TEACHER   The nominees for queen of Fling of Spring:
      Regina George and Gretchen Wieners, both,
      Then Janis Ian—

REGINA   [*aside:*]   —What is happening?
            Hath all the world gone senseless in a trice?   70
DAMIAN   [*to Janis:*] Ha! Thou art chosen by my trickery—
            'Tis well that I did man the ballot box.
            I could not help myself, 'twas eas'ly done!
TEACHER   The final nominee is Cady Heron.
                                        [*Exit teacher.*
CADY   O, Damian, what ruses hast thou plied?   75
            'Twas not within our plan for me to garner
            A vote to be the queen of Fling of Spring.
DAMIAN   'Twas not my work, I tell thee honestly.
CADY   The nomination hath been justly won?
JANIS   [*to Damian:*] Look how she smiles, much like a
                                        blushing bride. 80
                                [*Exeunt all but Cady.*
CADY   More time did pass as Fling of Spring approach'd.
            In January, thin Regina did
            Place holds upon a gown for the event,
            At an exclusive store nam'd One-Three-Five.
            Because she is a Plastic, she requir'd   85
            Advice from all the rest of us, her friends,
            Ere she could purchase it as she desir'd.

Enter REGINA GEORGE, *in a tight dress, with* GRETCHEN WIENERS,
        KAREN SMITH, *and a* SALESPERSON.

REGINA   Pray, someone zip the zipper on the gown,
            Then zip your mouths as ye do gape and judge.
                                [*Karen tries to zip Regina's dress.*
KAREN   It shall not close—the garment is too tight.   90
REGINA   It is a five, already large enow!

GRETCHEN   'Tis, peradventure, mark'd with errant size.

REGINA   Say, Cady, how this end hath come to pass?
The only morsels that do cross my lips
Are Kälteen bars, which thou hast given me.   95
They do not work.

CADY   —They do! Yet 'tis a process—
What thou experienc'st is part of it.
This is thy water weight that fills the gown—
Thou shalt bloat first, then drop a stone entire.
The Kälteen bars have burn'd thy nasty carbs,   100
Resulting in a body run by water.
When ev'ry drop of water in thee flees,
Thou shalt be naught but muscle, mark my words.
'Tis all explain'd upon the Swedish label.

REGINA   Thou speakest Swedish? This I did not know.   105

CADY   'Tis plain—for ev'ryone from Afric come
Is fluent in the way of Swedish words.

KAREN   [*to salesperson:*] I bid thee, madam, hast this one size
                                             up?
Another gown that better suits my friend?

SALESP.   Apologies, for we are limited—   110
We carry sizes one and three and five;
This is a store for slender women only.
Mayhap thou shouldst try Sears, along the road—
Its softer side may suit thy softer sides.

REGINA   Fie, fie! I'll not endure this treatment vile.   115

                               [*Exeunt Cady, Regina,*
                               Gretchen, and Karen.

SALESP.   From women's eyes this doctrine I derive:
They sparkle still the right Promethean fire;
They are the books, the arts, the academes,

That show, contain, and nourish all the world:
Else none at all in ought proves excellent.   120
Alas, when women's eyes look on themselves,
They either see a haggard, ugly hag,
When they should see true beauty in their face,
Or else, like this young lass, they too much value
The figure that shall one day be disfigur'd,   125
Which vanisheth an 'twere the morning new.
How I do love to make a woman doubt
The body over which she is devout.

                                        [Exit salesperson.

SCENE 5

*At North Shore High School over
several days the following week.*

Enter CADY HERON *and* MADAM NORBURY.

NORBURY   Ah, Cady, I had hop'd to speak with thee.
                        [Madam Norbury holds out a sheet of paper.
              Thy parents must their marks make hereunto,
              Acknowledging, by signature, that they
              Accept and are aware that thou are failing.

CADY   What, failing? I am like a helpless roe,   5
              Caught in a net and trapp'd while standing versus
              A river over which I cannot wade!

NORBURY   The circumstance is not sans irony:

	When thou dost take examinations, Cady,	
	The work is admirable and correct—	10
	Thou solvest ev'ry problem perfectly—	
	Yet somehow all thine answers, still, are problems.	
CADY	Indeed?	
NORBURY	—Indeed. I know a paramour	
	Doth seem as if 'tis urgent in th'extreme.	
	Yet if thou learnest aught from me, learn this:	15
	Thou shouldst not hide thy vast intelligence	
	To win some lad or make him think thee winsome.	
CADY	[*aside:*] A teacher speaking so? How would she know?	
NORBURY	I'll warrant thou dost wonder how would I know—	
	In love unlucky, recently divorc'd,	20
	And poor from being recently divorc'd.	
	The only man who calleth on me now	
	Is randy Randy ringing from Chase Visa!	
	Dost thou know wherefore this hath come to be?	
	Forsooth: I am a pusher; I push people.	25
	My husband, first, to law school did I push—	
	'Twas nothing but a bust of busted hopes—	
	At three careers I push'd myself to work,	
	And this same progeny of evils comes	
	From our debate, from our dissension, too;	30
	We are their parents and original.	
	Yet I shall push once more, though I should learn	
	The honey'd flavor of humility,	
	The essence sweet of one who pusheth not.	
	'Tis thou whom I shall push, good Cady, thou—	35
	Because I know thou smarter art than this.	
CADY	Your speech hath honor'd me and mov'd me, too—	
	My thanks to you, kind Madam Norbury.	

If extra credit I may somehow earn,
Pray tell me and it shall be done anon.   40

NORBURY   Indeed I shall, thou hast my solemn word.

                [Exit Madam Norbury.

Enter REGINA GEORGE, GRETCHEN WIENERS,
and KAREN SMITH.

REGINA   What words had Madam Norbury for thee?
For we did watch thee speak to her at length.

CADY   I do despise the woman utterly!
She plans to grade me low, whate'er I do,   45
Because I did not join her Mathlete crew.
The lady was quite queer in the exchange—
"I am a pusher, Cady," she did say,
"I am a pusher utterly."

REGINA   —Ha, ha!

KAREN   What doth it mean, that she a pusher is?   50

GRETCHEN   Perhaps like one who pusheth drugs? Is't so?

CADY   Belike 'tis, Gretchen. Yea, most probably,
For she declar'd she worketh at three jobs.
'Tis probable she selleth drugs to students
To supplement her meager teaching wages   55
And pay for her pathetic, sad divorce.

              [Gretchen pulls out the Burn Book.

GRETCHEN   Thine ev'ry thought and feeling thou canst write—
Put it inside the book and free thy soul.

              [Cady takes the book and
                begins to write in it.

CADY   *[aside:]* It seemeth I become a heartless hag,
Yet 'tis an act—a role I play—no more,   60

'Tis merely pretense of a heartless hag.
Although I write herein, pray, judge me not.
[*To the others:*] My thanks, kind friends. Farewell,
                     until the next.
           [*Gretchen takes the book. Exeunt Regina,*
                   Gretchen, and Karen.

Enter JANIS IAN *and* DAMIAN.

JANIS	Holla, kind Caddy. I have search'd for thee.
	Last night I call'd on thee; thou answer'd not. 65
	Say wherefore didst thou not return the call?
CADY	Too busy was I, past all thought or measure.
JANIS	As sure as I have a thought or a soul,
	Methought thou wouldst respond when I did call.
	No matter, though. Wilt thou require a ride 70
	Unto my art show when the weekend comes?
CADY	Alas, my time is to my parents sworn,
	With whom I must to Madison be ta'en.
	Apologies—I long'd to see thy show.
JANIS	[*aside:*] The quick excuse rings hollow and unkind— 75
	'Twould have been gentler simply to refuse.
DAMIAN	What of tonight? Wilt watch a film withal?
CADY	Nay, not this even. Major sabotage
	Of Plastics shall I undertake tonight.
JANIS	How canst thou ply this sabotage sans us? 80
	Are we not thy companions in the cause?
	Wilt thou desert thy friends so utterly?
	We had, tonight, plann'd nothing in our schemes.
CADY	Here I fly solo, like a pilot rogue—
	This plan is mine and shall be mine alone. 85

[The bell rings.
Farewell. Go with my heartfelt love, kind friends.
[Exit Cady, blowing a kiss.

DAMIAN   Am I deceiv'd or doth this strange goodbye
          Reek utterly of rank Regina's scent?
          Hath Cady's fake plasticity turn'd real?
          Is she condemn'd to be the Plastics' next?   90

JANIS   Whate'er this doth portend, all is not well.
          Shall we two lose a friend so newly won?
                         [Exeunt Janis and Damian.

Enter CADY HERON *above, on balcony, on the phone.*
Enter REGINA GEORGE *below, talking to her. Enter* GRETCHEN
WIENERS, *hidden, listening on the phone.*

CADY   Regina, thou shalt hear what did befall:
          Our Gretchen doth believe thou art upset
          Because she hath been nominated for   95
          The queen of Fling of Spring, which else is thine.

REGINA   Me, angry, Cady? Nay, it ne'er could be—
          Concern'd am I for her well-being only.
          Methinks her nomination is a jest,
          Some ruthless trick plied by a jealous fiend.   100
          When no one votes for her it would be best
          Put finger in the eye, an she knew why.
          She shalt melt down and reckless shall become.
          Who, then, shall care for her? It shall be I—
          Employment in this field appealeth not.   105

CADY   Thou dost not think she'll garner e'en one vote?

REGINA   The truth is, Cady: Gretchen is not fair.
          Why, then, should any vote for her as queen?

The truth e'er has the frightful, clanging sound
Of cymbals harshly beat by toddler hands—   110
Yet truth will out, however loud the noise.
The queen of Fling of Spring is ever gorgeous;
'Twill not be Gretchen for that very reason.
If there were any justice at our school,
Perchance sweet Karen would the honor earn.   115
Yet no one e'er has Karen on their minds,
For she is wanton as the grass is green.
Now, I have kept thee long enow, indeed,
And must to bed, to take my beauty sleep.

[Exit Regina, hanging up.

CADY   Come forward, Gretchen, thou hast heard the whole: 120
              She is not mad at thee, if 'tis some comfort.

GRETCHEN   Hold briefly.

CADY   —Art thou well?

GRETCHEN   —Pray, Cady, soft!
                                    [Gretchen calls Karen.

Enter KAREN SMITH, *on the phone.*

KAREN   Although I was inspecting my backside,
              As is my wont when eventide doth come,
              The ringing phone hath call'd to me. *[Into phone:]*
                                                  Hello?   125

GRETCHEN   If someone spake ill words about thee, Karen,
              Thou wouldst insist that I tell thee. 'Tis true?

KAREN   Nay.

GRETCHEN   —Even if the someone were thy friend?
              Or else, a person who did act as such?

KAREN   What art thou asking? O, the other line   130

Doth ring—I bid thee wait, whilst I make answer.

[Karen switches to another line.

GRETCHEN   [*to Cady:*] I shall not take this anymore!

CADY   —Good, Gretch!

I'd see thee whole, no more abusèd so.

KAREN   Holla?

Enter REGINA GEORGE, *on the phone with* KAREN.

REGINA   —Let us make merry with the night.

If thou shalt go along, we two shall frolic.   135

KAREN   We shall! Yet Gretchen holds upon the line.

REGINA   Invite her not; the lass doth drive me mad.

KAREN   Hold, then.

REGINA   —Make haste!

KAREN   [*to Gretchen:*]   —Regina 'tis who call'd.

She would the town paint red with me tonight,

And did instruct me not to tell thee so.   140

GRETCHEN   An thou dost love me, go thou not withal.

KAREN   Yet wherefore?

GRETCHEN   —Thou wouldst not the answer hear.

KAREN   O, tell me, then! But hold thou first, I pray.

*[Karen tries to address Regina
but speaks to Gretchen.*

By God, the lady doth annoy me so.

GRETCHEN   Who doth?

KAREN   —Who is this?

GRETCHEN   —Gretchen, as thou know'st. 145

KAREN   Of course, as I do know. Pray, hold the line.

[*To Regina:*] By God, the lady doth annoy me so.

REGINA   How well I know the truth of these thy words.

Release her now, that we may fly anon.

KAREN   [*to Gretchen:*] What is it thou wouldst tell me,

                                        Gretchen? Speak. 150

GRETCHEN   Regina said that no one liketh thee

Because thou art a shameless, wanton whore.

KAREN   These were her words?

GRETCHEN   —Thou heard'st it not from me.

CADY   'Twas harshly spoken, Gretchen.

GRETCHEN   —By my troth,

She hath the right to know what hath been said.   155

It is deserv'd; Regina's only gift

Is to devise impossible, harsh slanders,

And none but libertines delight in her.

                              [*Exeunt Cady and Gretchen.*

KAREN   Alas, Regina, I cannot go out.

Cough, cough—I am unwell, as thou canst hear.   160

REGINA   Boo, whore.

                                        [*Exit Regina.*

KAREN   —The words fall from the horse's mouth!

What devil art that dost torment me thus?

This torture should be roar'd in dismal hell.

Though I am not intelligent, I'd not

Receive such scorn. I may not be a smart lass,   165

But I know what love is. It is not this.

                                        [*Exit Karen.*

Enter CADY HERON *in the school cafeteria the next day.*

CADY   The revelations that came yesternight

Shall surely shape our conversation when

Our group doth share our luncheon presently.

Enter REGINA GEORGE, *sitting with* CADY. *Enter* GRETCHEN WIENERS
and KAREN SMITH *severally. Enter other* STUDENTS.

GRETCHEN	Regina, we would speak with thee at once.	170
REGINA	[*to Cady:*] Is butter such as may be call'd a carb?	
CADY	Indeed. [*Aside:*] Eat thou each stick upon the earth.	
GRETCHEN	Regina, thou in sweatpants art array'd!	
	'Tis Monday.	
REGINA	—And?	
KAREN	—Thou hast transgress'd our rules,	
	And art not welcome to be seated here.	175
REGINA	Whate'er! The rules ye broadcast are not real,	
	But are like morning fog that dissipates	
	When light of day doth break upon the ether.	
KAREN	Thou call'd them true when I did wear a vest.	
REGINA	A vest that was disgusting to mine eyes.	180
GRETCHEN	[*yelling:*] Thou mayst not, shalt not, canst not sit withal!	

REGINA   These sweatpants are the only garments that
                 Will fit the fuller body I have bred.
                 [*Aside:*] Humiliating revelation this!
                 Yet still they are not mov'd to show compassion.   185
                 [*To all:*] I shall depart, an ye shall have it so.
                 Walk home, you wenches—I shall drive thee not.

                             [*Regina stands to walk away*
                             and bumps into Student 8.

STUD. 8   Watch where thou goest, oafish lump of fat.
                   [*All laugh. Exit Regina in dismay.*

GRETCHEN   [*to Cady:*] What shall we do this weekend?

KAREN   —Tell us, what?

CADY   Alas, my time is to my parents sworn,   190
                 With whom I must to Madison be ta'en.

GRETCHEN   What? Do not leave us! We are lost sans thee.

CADY   They purchas'd tickets to some grand event.

KAREN   What, Cady? Shalt thou leave us all alone—
                 The sole remaining prop of our young age?   195

CADY   [*aside:*] See how they follow me, like wayward sheep.
                 Have I become the new queen bee to them,
                 And they my workers who would do my will?
                 Have I my stinger hon'd and form'd this hive?
                 [*To Karen:*] Perchance I can escape mine obligation.   200

KAREN   O, do, for our sake!

GRETCHEN   —Take our many thanks!

KAREN   Be well, kind Cady, till we meet again.

                     [*Exeunt Gretchen and Karen and other*
                               students.

CADY   How shall I tell my parents of this plan?
                 The trip to Madison is not untrue—
                 I fear they'll be dismay'd if I refuse.   205

Enter LADY HERON *and* SIR HERON.

Beseech you, Father, Mother, hear my plea:
May I stay home from Madison this weekend?
My comrade Janis hath an art show then—
I would attend it, show her my support.

LADY H.   The tickets we did purchase months ago,   210
And thou dost love Ladysmith Black Mambazo.

CADY   She is my friend, and I have giv'n my word.

SIR H.   Methinks our Cady hath grown old enow
That she one night without us may endure.
The flower kept too much protected shall   215
Ne'er learn to flourish by the sun's bright light.

CADY   O, Father, many thanks I give to thee!

SIR H.   Thou art our daughter and doth have our love.
                    [Exeunt Lady Heron and Sir Heron.

CADY   Have I discover'd how I may control
Each person I encounter in my life?   220
Shall I turn wizard, witch, or sorcerer
That I, by magic, move the minds of all?
This might is daunting and intoxicating.
There's Aaron coming hither presently,
As if he were by heav'nly power sent!   225

Enter AARON SAMUELS.

Brave Aaron, I have miss'd thy company.
Most gladly, though, it shall not bring us woe:
This weekend I shall host a revelry—
Wilt thou be present?

AARON   —Shall Regina go?

CADY   Nay, I have made of her no such request.   230
                Think'st thou, mayhap, that Cady hath gone mad?
                The gathering consisteth of the best—
                Good people; thou shalt to that number add.

AARON   'Tis well. I shall attend.

CADY   —Tut, tut, thou egg.
                Thy tunic's masterfully woven, too.   235
                O think that not an afterthought, I beg!
                Until the party, I bid thee adieu.

                                        [Exit Aaron.

                The soldiers are arrang'd, the plan in motion:
                My sweet lieutenant, Aaron Samuels, shall
                Report for duty to my parents' house.   240
                All must be perfect, if I'd win this war.
                My uniform must be most fashionable,
                That when he sees me, he'll surrender quickly.
                If it proves so, then loving goes by haps:
                Some Cupids kill with arrows, some with traps.   245

                                        [Exit Cady.

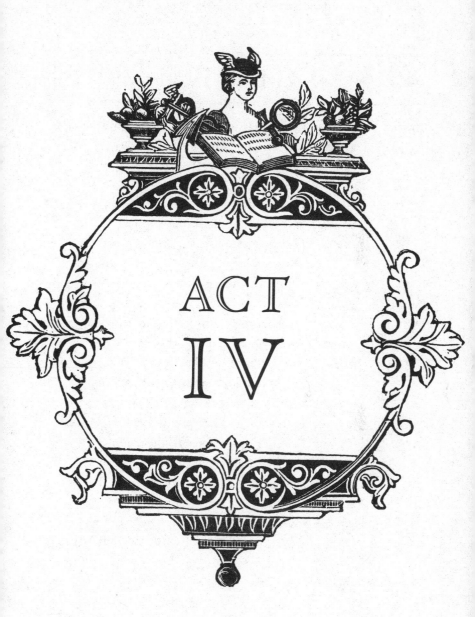

ACT
IV

SCENE 1

The Heron residence.

Enter GRETCHEN WIENERS *and* KAREN SMITH.

GRETCHEN   The first ball held at Cady's parents' house!
                How fortunate we are to be her friends.

KAREN   Indeed! The luckiest of women we!

Enter CADY HERON.

CADY   O, welcome, friends! Your outfits are supreme
          And fit for any palace, hall, or court.   5
          This night we'll hold within our mem'ries. O!
          We'll have no more of slander, fraud, or con,
          We shall be harpies neither, gossips nor.

GRETCHEN   Thou art so wise, and beautifully attir'd!

CADY   I am! 'Tis not a boast when 'tis the truth.   10
          Tonight, I have secur'd a block of cheese
          And wafers plentiful enow for eight.
          Think ye that such a total shall suffice?

GRETCHEN   [*aside:*] We have invited many more than eight,
          Yet I would not upset good Cady. [*To Cady:*] Yea!   15

Enter many STUDENTS *to the party, including*
JASON, TAYLOR WEDELL, *and* KEVIN GNAPOOR.

CADY   'Tis not enow, as now I plainly see—
          The word of our small gathering hath been

	Announc'd unto the world, as by a herald	
	Proclaiming some glad news of an event,	
	The tidings whereof all the folk would hear.	20

GRETCHEN   My Jason is arriv'd, but comes with Taylor,
            She of the cursèd family Wedell.

KAREN   He doth but use the wench to drive thee mad.

CADY   'Mongst all who hither come, have ye seen Aaron?

JASON   The music in this house is wondrous strange—   25
            Let's play the Ramayana Monkey Chant!

> *[The doorbell rings.*

CADY   [*aside:*] Who are these people ringing at the door?
            A newfound group I do not recognize.

Enter more STUDENTS *to the party.*

            Do I know ye, who unfamiliar art?

STUD. 9   [*seeing a student inside:*] Good Deek, thou dog!

CADY   [*aside:*]   —So burly
                                          and so odd.   30
            'Tis not the gathering I did intend,
            For did my parents know, they would be wroth.

Enter REGINA GEORGE *and* SHANE OMAN, *outside the house.*

REGINA   Doth she imagine she shall hold a party,
            Inviting ev'ry student save myself?
            It shall not be—I am Regina George,   35
            And, like my namesake, stand as queen o'er all.
            What pretense doth she ply, to be so bold?

SHANE   Thou hast it right, my fragile, fragrant flow'r.

REGINA   'Tis not absurd to say I made her—aye,

Just as the potter makes the jar of clay,   40
And may—an she so willeth—smash it, too.
Fie!

Enter AARON SAMUELS *to the party.*

AARON   [*aside:*] —Marry, 'tis an unexpected scene.
Methought 'twould be a gath'ring intimate,
With Cady and a few companions only.
My prior expectations I'll adjust—   45
I may still author lines to sway the crowd.
                              [*Gretchen approaches Jason.*

GRETCHEN   Dissembling Jason, may I speak a word?
                              [*Gretchen falls, intoxicated.*

TAYLOR   This drama is too rich a spectacle—
I shall not be an actor on this stage.
                    [*Exit Taylor. Gretchen starts to arise.*

GRETCHEN   I love thee, Jason, heartily.

JASON   —I know.   50
Pray rest thy head and heart in me, my dove.
               [*Two students begin playing catch with a vase.*

CADY   Pray, set that down, for 'tis a priceless vase!
[*Aside:*] O, where is Aaron? Hath he turn'd me down?
Shall I read absence as rejection total?
Another drink shall steel my worried nerves.   55
                              [*Cady sips her drink.*

KEVIN   Good evening, Africa, how dost thou fare?
Thy friend, e'en Gretchen Wieners, told me all—
With thee I'll share the product of our discourse.

CADY   [*aside:*] Alas, hath Gretchen slyly told him of
Some false infatuation of my heart?   60

KEVIN   While I am flatter'd by thine interest,

It must be circumscrib'd ere it expands.

When romance adds a lass unto my life,

She shall be someone bless'd with vivid hues—

To put it plain: thy palette is too white.   65

CADY   Thy words do move—

KEVIN   —Thine undivided heart?

CADY   My bladder; I must urinate anon.

                                  [Exit Kevin.

My house entire is overrun and wild,

Each room suffus'd with hormones, japes, and fools.

In this one, here is Gretchen kissing Jason,   70

As if they hop'd to make their faces one.

Yet, as I enter, Gretchen sees me here

And slappeth him, continuing their show.

                      [Cady enters her room.

Here is another room, mine own, indeed—

[*To two students:*] Be gone, I tell ye, I must take my

                                      rest.   75

                 [Cady walks aside within her room.

                      Regina enters the party.

REGINA   I'll find the base, deceiving little harpy,

Hiding her bitter jests in blunt behavior.

                 [Cady walk aside into her bathroom.

AARON   [*aside:*] Regina! I had hop'd she'd not be here.

I'll make escape and hide me in a trice.

                     [Aaron enters Cady's room.

A party too unruly for my taste—   80

This room shall be a refuge for my mind.

'Tis Cady's, if mine eyes deceive me not,

For these her garments are, and these her portraits,

The marks and wonders of her private sphere.
This photograph—the Plastics, one and all,   85
With Cady's lovely visage in a scowl,
As if she'd learn'd Regina's ev'ry move.
Behind it, though, another, better scene:
Young Cady, as a child, astride a beast,
An elephant of monstrous girth and weight,   90
Which holds its trunk aloft with mighty bray,
And almost smiles—if elephants may smile—
As though it knew what precious, charming cargo
It carried on its ample, potent back.
Sweet Cady, innocent and still a girl,   95
With hair in tails and knees unkempt with dirt,
Doth beam like one who ne'er was happier.
This is the Cady whom I've come to love,
Not she who is but plastic, fake, and cruel.
                    [Cady comes back into her room.

AARON	Holla, kind Cady.
CADY	—Aaron come! But how? 100
AARON	Most ev'rywhere throughout the house I search'd,
	Yet could not find thee anywhere till now.
CADY	For thee I look'd as well, I leap'd and lurch'd.
AARON	Thy garments are a banquet for the eyes—
	Hast thou obtain'd them lately? Are they new? 105
CADY	My thanks, thy compliment is sweet surprise.
AARON	Shall we downstairs, the party to pursue?
CADY	With thee, herein, I'd happily remain.

                    [She pulls him to the bed, where they both sit.

AARON	Thanks for the invitation for tonight.
CADY	'Tis pleasure to have thee in my domain. 110
AARON	Too long I've let Regina blind my sight,

	Mine anger over her hath work'd me woe.	
	No more would I have liars in my life.	
CADY	Ne'er would I lie to thee, as thou must know.	
AARON	Indeed I do; ne'er couldst thou bring me strife.	115
CADY	Although, one word of falsehood I'll admit—	
	I'll warrant thou shalt laugh at the confession.	
AARON	What is it?	
CADY	—I did feign to be unfit	
	At mathematics, though 'tis my obsession.	
	'Twas done because I hop'd I'd win thy favor.	120
	Yet, truly, I'm not bad at math, but smart.	
	The truth is like fine wine that one may savor—	
	I am quite skill'd at math, more than thou art!	
	The situation grows yet funnier,	
	For now at mathematics I am failing.	125
AARON	This problem must, in time, grow sunnier.	
	Thou fail'st on purpose? Foolishness prevailing!	
CADY	It was not purposeful, nay, by my troth,	
	Yet gave me reason for to speak with thee.	
AARON	Next time I bid thee—yea, make thou an oath:	130
	Whenever thou desirest, talk to me.	
CADY	Nay, I could not, due to Regina George.	
	She stak'd her claim an 'twere a property.	
AARON	Her property? No shackles did she forge.	
CADY	Shut up thy mouth—	
AARON	—Nay, it may never be!	135
CADY	Apologies, I did not mean to say—	
AARON	By heaven, this is worse than I had thought.	
	Thou art too much in mean Regina's sway,	
	As if thou wert a clone that she had wrought.	
CADY	Nay, listen, Aaron, thou dost not hear well.	140

[*Aside:*] Alas, it cometh—vomit in my words.
Nay, not in words—O torment come from hell!
                              [*Regina enters Cady's room.*

REGINA   What is this scene?
CADY   [*aside:*]   —Real vomit, come in herds!
                    [*Cady vomits on Aaron. Aaron begins to leave.*
                    Exeunt all except Cady as she pursues Aaron
                              outside the front door of the house.
             O, Aaron, wait! Call on me soon, my sweet.

             Enter JANIS IAN *and* DAMIAN *outside the house,*
                    driving by in Damian's car.

             [*Aside:*] Alas, 'tis Janis, whom I did betray.   145
JANIS   Thou dirty, lying knave.
CADY   —I shall explain!
JANIS   Explain how thou didst somehow quite forget
             To give thy friends an invitation, eh?
             Friends are not for forgetting, Cady, nay,
             And parties are where thou shouldst want us most.   150
DAMIAN   The car's progression, Janis, I'll not stop—
             I durst not flout the curfew from my parents.
CADY   You know that I could not invite ye here—
             My duty 'twas, pretending to be Plastic.
JANIS   No pretense 'tis. Nay, 'tis reality.   155
             Thou Plastic art: cold, shiny, and unbending.
DAMIAN   My curfew's one—the time turns to one ten.
JANIS   Thy and thine awesome, newfound friends withal—
             Did ye enjoy yourselves, I wonder? Ha!
             Did ye drink alcohol that pleas'd your minds?   160
             Did ye play music that amus'd your souls?

	Did ye bask in each other's awesomeness?
CADY	Thou art the one who made me as I am,
	To use me for thine overdue revenge,
	Which thou didst cling to from an eighth-grade
	slight. 165
JANIS	At least Regina George and I do know
	That we are vicious, mean, and spiteful, too.
	Thou dost pretend thou art an innocent—
	"I liv'd in Afric," thou dost gladly claim,
	"The birdies and the monkeys were my friends!" 170
CADY	'Tis not my fault thou art in love with me.
JANIS	What madness?
DAMIAN	—Say she did not speak those words.
JANIS	'Tis what you Plastics do with utmost skill:
	Ye think the world enamor'd of yourselves,
	When 'tis far truer ye are hated widely. 175
	Take Aaron Samuels, whom thou fawnest for—
	He broke with his Regina. Nonetheless,
	He still doth not regard thee with love's eye.
	Then wherefore dost thou meddle with Regina?
	Here is the reason: thou a mean girl art— 180
	A wench, a strumpet, and a soulless rogue!

[Janis throws a rolled-up painting at Cady.

	Take thou this portrait, for I want it not—
	It won a prize that now turns sour to me.
	Fie on it! I am gone, though I am here:
	There is no love in thee. [*To Damian:*] Pray, let us go. 185
DAMIAN	My tunic pink, thou must return to me!

[Exeunt Janis and Damian.
Cady unrolls the portrait.

| CADY | Her portrait doth convict, an 'twere a judge. |

Herein I see we three most happy friends—
Myself, kind Janis, we with Damian,
As if we were three tight-knit musketeers,   190
Inseparable as the trinity.
O, how I have behav'd—or misbehav'd—
The friendship they did freely proffer me
I have return'd at best derisively.
Have I become the evil I deplore?   195
Forgive me, friends; I shall yet make this right.

                         [Exit Cady.

Enter REGINA GEORGE *and* SHANE OMAN, *approaching Regina's car.*

SHANE	I prithee, calm thyself. Be thou not so fierce.
REGINA	Existeth anyone I still may trust?

                     [Regina begins to eat a Kälteen bar.

SHANE	Why eatest thou a Kälteen bar, Regina?
REGINA	My stomach feeleth famish'd, verily. 200
	To be betray'd is hungry work, indeed.
SHANE	Those bars are most despicable to me.
	Coach Carr gives them to us when he desires
	That we increase our weight class for the team.
REGINA	What didst thou say?
SHANE	—They swiftly boost one's weight 205
	And add onto one's girth. Perchance to eat
	Pure fat would better work, yet not by much.
REGINA	Fie, fie, O monstrous, common-kissing lout!
	That artless, lumpish, motley-minded flirt-gill!

                     [Exit Shane in dismay.

        What, will none suffer me? Nay, now I see   210
        She is the treasure, she must have a boyfriend;

I must dance barefoot on her wedding day
And for her sake to her lead apes in hell.
               [Regina finds the Burn Book in her car.
Where is the Burn Book I have lately scorn'd?
It shall fulfill my purpose presently.   215
Revenge shall be most swift and terrible—
The world entire shall know how rank she is.
Let it be writ: "This girl's a skanky whore,
The nastiest whom ever I have met.
Trust her no wise—she fugly is forsooth!"   220
These words, however, I pen not of her—
But place my picture underneath the words.
Thus shall the book become a Cady share,
Wherewith I'll ruin her beyond repair.
                       [Exit Regina.

SCENE 2

At North Shore High School.

Enter SIR DUVALL.

DUVALL   In all my dreaming, never did I think
I someday would be in a school employ'd.
Though as schoolmaster I expend my days,
In other meadows I would gladly frolic.
I could be principal of a brigade,   5
Engag'd all day in soldierly pursuits.

I could be principal upon the stage,
An actor playing in a leading role.
I could be principal within a choir,
A tenor who doth make the ladies swoon.   10
Yet here I sit, schoolmaster to the many,
Most unappreciated for mine efforts.

Enter REGINA GEORGE, *crying and holding the Burn Book.*

REGINA   Wise Sir Duvall, I bid you give me aid.
            I found this book, whose pages hurt me so.
            'Twas in the ladies' restroom. 'Tis so vile—   15
            A wicked, heartless tome infus'd with slander.
                          [Sir Duvall begins reading the book.

DUVALL   Are these words true? Heav'n help me if they are—
            Hath young Trang Pak been kissing our Coach Carr?
            What here is written? "Kaitlyn Caussin is a—"

REGINA   "Fat whore." At least, I do believe 'tis so.   20
            O, horrible, that one should be so cruel!

DUVALL   Pray, calm thyself, Miss George. All is not lost.

REGINA   Yet wherefore would a person write those words?
            They are mean-spirited beyond belief.

DUVALL   Fear not, we shall not rest until 'tis right,   25
            And shall discover where the blame doth rest.

REGINA   If you would read precisely, Sir Duvall,
            You shall find but three lasses in the school
            Who are not mention'd in the horrid pages.
            [*Aside:*] The trap is set and, for the final act,   30
            I'll set the school afire in rage and bile.
                                      [Exit Regina.

Enter COACH CARR, CADY HERON,
and various STUDENTS *above, on balcony, in class.*

CARR   At your age, how thy bodies start to burn
With primal urges uncontrollable.
You shall desire to cast aside thy garments
And touch each other in your hidden parts.   35
If ye do so, chlamydia shall follow—
Which doth, like plague, lead instantly to death.

Enter a MESSENGER.

MESS.   Coach Carr? A written note hath come for thee,
Sent by our noble Sir Duvall's strong hand.
        [Exit messenger. Coach Carr reads the note.

CARR   Thou, Cady Heron, art requir'd anon,   40
Within the office of the principal.

CADY   [*aside:*] To Sir Duvall at once I'm bound to sally,
And gladly leave this classroom for the ride.
Of visits to his office 'tis my first—
Doth this denote my own growth as a woman?   45
Or, likely, I am simply wanted in
Some hap for which my brain hath not the space.
        [Exit Cady.

CARR   Back to chlamydia, where we did stop.
'Tis K-L-A-M-I-D-D-E-A.
        [Exeunt Coach Carr and students from balcony.

Enter CADY HERON.

CADY   [*aside:*] Was that Regina I saw walking past?   50

             The look she gave me could infernos freeze.
DUVALL   This way, Miss Heron, to my office, please.

Enter GRETCHEN WIENERS *and* KAREN SMITH *in* SIR DUVALL'*s office.*

CADY   What is the matter? Gladly would I know.
DUVALL   I bid thee sit, and thou shalt learn anon.
                        [Sir Duvall holds up the Burn Book.
             Hast thou e'er seen this wretched book before?   55
CADY   Nay. Well, not nay. I have. Yet 'tis not mine.
             I once was reader—never author, though.
DUVALL   Thy story's not well told, Miss Heron, nay—
             There is the sound of fiction in the telling,
             And I do not enjoy fallacious tales.   60
GRETCHEN   'Tis not ours, but Regina's, Sir Duvall.
             She'd have you think we three did hold the pen,
             Which, in this case, cuts deeper than the sword,
             Yet 'tis her work in ev'ry jot and tittle.
DUVALL   Why would Regina "fugly" call herself,   65
             And "skanky whore"—Miss Wieners, canst thou say?
                               [Karen laughs.
             This is no time for jests and japes, Miss Smith.
             We shall uncover this at one fell swoop,
             Ere we do leave this office. Do ye hear?

Enter REGINA GEORGE, *aside, spreading papers around the hallways.*

REGINA   The perfect end unto the perfect plot—   70
             These copies of my treasur'd folio
             Shall spread around the school an 'twere a wildfire.
             Self-publishing was ne'er so gratifying.

[Exit Regina.

GRETCHEN   Belike we are not in the volume harsh
Because we are belov'd of ev'ryone.   75
'Twould not be proper if you punish'd me
But for the phony crime of being lik'd.
My father, he who Toaster Strudel did
Invent, would not be pleas'd to hear of it.

The bell rings. Enter STUDENTS, *including* JANIS IAN, DAMIAN, JASON,
DAWN SCHWEITZER, TRANG PAK, *and* SUN JIN DINH, *aside, in the
hallways, discovering* REGINA's *papers.*

STUD. 10   What is this defamation? "Kiss'd a hot dog!"   80
'Twas one time only, not a daily act!
DAWN   "Dawn Schweitzer hath a monstrous, braying ass."
Who would such mean and hurtful words compose?
STUD. 11   Who would not write it of thee, by my troth!
[Dawn and Student 11 begin fighting.
JASON   "Trang Pak hath kiss'd Coach Carr"—can this be so?   85
"And so did Sun Jin Dinh," such gossip sweet!
*[Trang and Sun Jin begin fighting. Many other
groups of students begin fighting.*

Enter MADAM NORBURY. *Enter* COACH CARR *severally.*

NORBURY   What is this chaos? Settle down at once!
Push not, lest ye be push'd! And be ye—ow!
[Madam Norbury is knocked to the ground.
What is this pamphlet here upon the floor?
A note about myself, and portrait too?   90
"Our Madam Norbury a pusher is—

	A sad drug pusher is she!" O, alas!	
DUVALL	Have you three anything ye wish to say?	
GRETCHEN	No further questions shall I answer, yea,	
	Until a parent or a lawyer's present.	95
DUVALL	[*aside:*] The first thing we do, let's kill all the lawyers.	
	[*To Karen:*] Miss Smith?	
KAREN	—Whoe'er hath written it,	
	mayhap,	
	Bethought no eyes would ever read its leaves.	
DUVALL	We still may hope no one shall ever read it.	

Enter REGINA GEORGE, *amid the chaos in the school.*

REGINA	[*aside:*] A perfect conflagration by my hand.	100
	By this I trust I may have leave to speak,	
	And speak I will. I am no child, no babe:	
	My pen can tell the anger of my heart,	
	Or else my heart, concealing it, will break,	
	And rather than it shall, I will be free	105
	E'en to the uttermost through these, my words.	
DAMIAN	[*to Janis:*] Read this harsh sentence: "Janis Ian: dyke."	
JANIS	Originality is not a strength	
	Of whomsoever did devise this barb.	
DAMIAN	Wait, wait, here is another writ of me:	110
	"His gaiety doth overwhelm his sense!"	
JANIS	Unfair, indeed, thou art too much malign'd—	
	These words should only from my mouth go forth.	
	[*Students argue and fight further.*	
STUD. 12	Didst thou write this?	
STUD. 13	—Nay, never, so swear I!	
STUD. 14	Thou toldest someone?	

STUD. 15   —She did tell.

STUD. 16   —Cur!

STUD. 17   —Hag!   115

JASON   How I do love to see young women spar—
For better fisticuffs, take off your tunics!

DUVALL   Here, then, is what we'll do—

Enter JOAN, *assistant to* SIR DUVALL, *to his office.*

JOAN   [*to Sir Duvall:*]   —Ron, quickly come!
The girls fly to and fro—they run amok!
           [*Sir Duvall, carrying a bat, and Cady,*
           Gretchen, and Karen emerge from the office
           into the hallway. Coach Carr is stuck
           between Trang and Sun Jin.

CADY   [*aside:*] 'Tis madness ev'rywhere, like ne'er I saw!   120
A full-tilt jungle scene with animals!
Unlike I had imagin'd it before,
It doth not disappear when I do blink.

CARR   [*to Sir Duvall:*] I pull'd these two apart, lest they
                          should kill.

DUVALL   Coach Carr, step quickly from the underag'd.   125

CARR   Alas! I am undone. I beg your mercy!
           [*Exit Coach Carr in haste.*

DUVALL   [*to a student:*] Thou, who dost hang there from the
                          pipes above,
I'll help thee, if thou shalt, by me, be help'd.
           [*The student tries to kick Sir Duvall,*
           who moves away quickly.
By hell's dark fire, I was not made for this!
I did not leave the south side for this turmoil.   130

If they make fire, they'll have the remedy.
                    [*Sir Duvall smashes a fire alarm with his bat.*
                    Water begins falling on all students. All scream.
Ye junior women to the gym anon!
Immediately, sans delay or sound!
                                  [*Exeunt all save Sir Duvall.*
In all my dreaming, never did I think
I someday would be in a school employ'd.   135
Yet here I am, by reason or by rhyme—
I could be principal for such a time.
                                  [*Exit Sir Duvall.*

SCENE 3

In the North Shore High School gymnasium.

Enter CADY HERON, REGINA GEORGE, GRETCHEN WIENERS,
KAREN SMITH, MADAM NORBURY, JOAN, *all* TEACHERS,
and all FEMALE STUDENTS. *Enter* DAMIAN, *disguised.*

CADY   [*aside:*] Have you e'er happen'd on two people at
            The moment when they shar'd a gossip tourney,
            With you the subject? Here, 'tis general.
            And though I smile and sing a "fa" or "re,"
            'Tis noted that each face doth signal "no."   5
                        [*Cady waves at Janis and Damian,*
                                who both grimace.

JANIS   [*aside:*] Who doth she think she is, to wave so fondly?

Who doth she think we are, thus to forgive?

Enter Sir Duvall.

DUVALL	Ne'er in my fourteen years as educator
	Have I seen such behavior as ye show.
	Young ladies are ye, or so ye should be.
	Your parents call upon me to inquire,
	"Hath someone by a gunshot injur'd been?"
	Your Fling of Spring I should, abruptly, cancel,
	Since ye already fling your minds away
	And spring to violence with a ready will.
ALL	Nay, nay!
KAREN	[*aside to Gretchen:*]—What should we do, if he doth cancel?
DUVALL	I'll not do so, despite my reservations—
	Already hath the deejay been reserv'd.
	Think not, howe'er, this book's not serious,
	Or that by it I am not most upset.
	Coach Carr hath left school property in haste.
	He is compos'd and fram'd of treachery:
	And fled he is upon this villainy.
	Our Madam Norbury hath been accus'd
	Of selling drugs, though such is ludicrous.
	This school is hard enough without infighting.
	What you young women need is to remake
	Your attitudes, which shall begin e'en now.
	Whatever length of time the matter takes,
	However through the night we all must work—
JOAN	In sooth, we can't keep them past four o'clock.
NORBURY	However until four we all must work—

10

15

20

25

30

We'll stay and fix how ye communicate,
How you relate unto each other. See?
'Twill happen lass to lass. Who, then, shall start?   35
Who hath a lady's problem to discuss?
                              [*Bethany Byrd raises her hand.*
Yes, Bethany, how shalt thou lead herein?

BETHANY   Whoever wrote the book declar'd that I
Did lie about my maidenhead, because
I utilize the tampons jumbo-siz'd.   40
'Tis not my fault that I have heavy flow,
Withal a large, wide-set vagina, too.

DUVALL   I cannot do this. Madam Norbury?
Thou art a most successful, caring, graceful,
Intelligent, and lovely woman, yea.   45

NORBURY   Am I? Thy words describe not how I feel.

DUVALL   Canst thou not, in the calmer exc'lence of
Thy wisdom, reconcile it with thy heart
To say aught that shall ease our school's disorder?

NORBURY   What?

DUVALL   —Canst thou cheer them up? O, say thou canst,   50
Speak something to increase their self-esteem.

NORBURY   'Tis not a problem of their self-esteem—
It seemeth they are well pleas'd with themselves.

DUVALL   [*aside to her:*] I beg thee, please.

NORBURY   —I shall endeavor so.
Close ye your eyes, each lady hereabouts.   55
                              [*The students close their eyes.*
I bid ye, raise your hands if e'er a lass
Spake gossip rank of ye behind your back.
                              [*All students raise their hands.*
Ope ye your eyes and see who shares your plight.

See how your comrades suffer as you do?
Close eyes again and hear another question.   60
                              [*The students close their eyes.*
Raise hands once more if ever you have said
Some grievous ill about your friend as well.
                              [*All students raise their hands.*
Ope yet again, and share communal guilt.
See some are gossipers, some gossipees,
But ev'ryone hath fac'd a sister's slander.   65
There hath been girl-on-girl misconduct here.
Let us take time today for exercises,
Which, in the doing, shall give you some ways
T'express your anger in a healthy manner.
We shall begin at once, with ye girls here.   70
                              [*Madam Norbury approaches
                              some students, who begin talking
                              with one another.*

CADY   [*aside:*] With Madam Norbury assisting us,
            As Sherpa to our trying uphill climb,
            We each discuss some matters difficult—
            Whate'er hath bother'd us in recent months.
            Each clique, it seems, hath challenges unique.   75

STUD. 18   [*to Student 19:*] Thou hast been prideful since thou
                                        mad'st the switch
            Unto short fielder on the softball squad.
            Dawn, here, agrees withal.

STUD. 19   —Dawn, is this so?

DAWN   Drag me not down beneath your murky sea—
            I pitch tomorrow, would not sunken be.   80
            If our team doth not win, it is a shame,
            For 'tis one-two-three-out at th'old ball game.

TRANG   [*to Sun Jin:*]Why scammest thou upon my boyfriend
                                                    gentle?
           Fie, fie! You counterfeit, you puppet, you!

SUN JIN   Puppet? Why so? Aye, that way goes the game.   85
           Now I perceive that she hath made compare
           Between our statures; she hath urg'd her height.
           And art thou grown so high in thine esteem,
           Because I am so dwarfish and so low?
           Thou art but jealous that I am more lik'd.   90

TRANG   I have no gift at all in shrewishness.

NORBURY   This strange communication, if 'tis what
           Ye need, shall serve us well. Well done, good maids.

REGINA   [*rising:*] May I but speak? There is, within our school,
           No problem that was born by having cliques.   95
           Some of us, thereby, should not forcèd be
           To listen or be present at this workshop.
           Some of us are but victims of these crimes.

NORBURY   A point well ta'en, Miss George, and likely true:
           How many of ye here have pers'nally felt   100
           Ye have been victimized e'en by Regina?
                              [*All students except Regina raise
                               their hands, and all teachers, too.*

DUVALL   [*aside:*] Though it brings shame, I too must raise my
                                                          hand.

REGINA   [*aside:*] Sorrow on thee and all the pack of you,
           That triumph thus upon my misery!

NORBURY   'Tis well, thank ye for sharing honestly.   105
           Who shall be next in our discussion? Cady.
           Is there a matter thou wouldst here confess?

CADY   [*aside:*] I should say yea, but courage fails me. [*To
                              Madam Norbury:*] Nay.

NORBURY   Ne'er hast thou, whether by mishap or malice,
            A rumor launch'd concerning anyone?   110
CADY   [*aside:*] The truth doth burn—I said that thou sell'st
                                                        drugs!
            [*To Madam Norbury:*] Nay.
NORBURY   —Naught for which thou
                                        wouldst apologize?
CADY   [*aside:*] She doth not fathom my predicament:
            Were I to make apology to her,
            The Burn Book blame would fall on me at once.   115
            [*To Madam Norbury:*] Nay, nay, I say again, and shall
                                                    not change.
NORBURY   My disappointment in thee only grows.
            [*To all:*] We are drawn hither by this beastly book—
            I know not who would write so foul a thing,
            Yet ye must cease the cries of "whore!" and "slut!"   120
            Your actions give permission unto lads
            To call ye whores and speak of sluttery.
            Who here hath been accus'd of sluttishness?
                        [*Some students raise their hands,
                            including Karen, who smiles.*
            I bid ye stand to face the next pursuit.
                        [*Students stand, and teachers
                        hand them writing utensils and paper.*
CADY   [*aside:*] Now Madam Norbury shall have us write   125
            Apologies to people we have hurt.
            These shall we read aloud, then bravely fall
            Into the waiting arms of all our classmates.
                        [*Students gather around a platform. One
                        student at a time reads her apology, then falls
                        safely into the waiting arms of other students.*

STUD. 20   In friendship have I fail'd thee, kind Alyssa,
            Ne'er should have callèd thee a gap-tooth'd wench.   130
            'Tis not thy fault thy teeth are so widespread,
            An 'twere a vast canal betwixt two cliffs.

KAREN   Dear Gretchen, my apologies for laughing
            When thou with diarrhea wast beset
            At the booksellers in the hindmost section—   135
            E'en sorrier that I told ev'ryone,
            And sorry, too, that I retell it now.

STUD. 21   I hate thee not because thou art so fat,
            Kind Laura—thou art fat because I hate thee.

STUD. 22   Would that we could be friends, as we have been   140
            Back, once upon a time, in middle school.
            Would that I could create a luscious cake,
            Whose recipe doth call for smiles and rainbows,
            Which we would feast upon, and happy be.

DAMIAN   She doth not even go here!
NORBURY   —Verily?   145
            [to Student 22:] Art thou a student here at North
                                            Shore High?

STUD. 22   Nay, yet I have so many feelings.
NORBURY   —Go!
                                    [Exit Student 22.

DUVALL   [aside to Madam Norbury:] Wise Sharon, thou
                            comport'st thyself so well.

NORBURY   My thanks—it seems I somehow muddle through.

GRETCHEN   I'm sorry ye feel jealous when ye see me;   150
            'Tis not my fault that I am popular.
            If I do feign, you witnesses above
            Punish my life for tainting my self-love!
                    [Gretchen falls and no one catches her except

> *Karen. They both fall to the ground.*

NORBURY	Alas, what hath befallen! Ah, you two—
	Get up and walk a little, mend yourselves. 155
GRETCHEN	That hurt!
KAREN	—Alack!
NORBURY	—They shall be well enow.
	Who shall be next to tell their inmost truth?

> *[Cady is next in line.*
> *She begins to exit in embarrassment.*

JANIS	[*aside:*] I'll jump the line ere Cady flies away—
	She shall not 'scape before I've had my say.

> *[Janis mounts the platform.*

REGINA	By heaven, 'tis her greatest fantasy— 160
	A pile of girls in which to jump and play.
JANIS	Indeed, I have a frank apology.
	I have a new friend who is newly come—
	A North Shore High School novice verily—
	Whom I convinc'd it would be rather fun 165
	To make Regina George's life a mess.
	I bid her play a role in my deceit:
	To be Regina's friend and new sworn sister.
	She would spend stretches at Regina's side,
	Then to my house fly with the highest speed 170
	To tell me of the ire and foolishness
	That had escap'd from mean Regina's mouth.
	We then would laugh to hear the motley tales.
	Our counterfeit turn'd to malevolence—
	We gave Regina candy bars that made 175
	Her gain the weight that she would rather lose.
	We also turn'd her closest friends from her
	And caught them in our net of treachery.

My friend, this Cady, soon was trading kisses
With Aaron Samuels, once Regina's love,   180
And then bid him to break up with Regina.
We, too, did give her foot cream, not face wash.
By Jove, I am so sorry, poor Regina.
I know not wherefore we have acted so.
Belike 'tis that I have a crush on thee—   185
A giant, Sapphic, lesbianic crush.
Methinks this kind confession suits thee well!
               [Janis jumps into the waiting
                   arms with a cry of victory.

ALL   Hurrah for Janis! Janis is our lass!
              [Regina walks out of the gymnasium

> *to the street, pursued by Cady.*
> *Regina crosses the street.*

CADY   Regina, wait! I bid thee, stop and hear!
                I did not wish upon thee this event.   190

REGINA   To hear the school entire doth hate me, eh?
                I do not care.

CADY   —Regina, prithee!
                [Regina turns back and approaches Cady in the
                street. Students and teachers emerge from the
                gymnasium to witness the scene.

REGINA   —Nay!
                Know'st thou what all do say about thee, Cady?
                They say thou art a homeschool'd jungle freak,
                Who is a less fair version of myself.   195
                Try not to act completely innocent!
                Instead, take thine apology absurd
                And shove it in thy hairy, hideous—
                    [A bus suddenly and forcefully strikes Regina.

CADY   O Fate, have you been watching over us—
                Hath justice been deliver'd by a bus?   200
                                        [Exeunt.

ACT
V

SCENE 1

At the Heron residence and North Shore High School.

Enter several STUDENTS, *singing a funeral dirge.*

STUDENTS   [*singing:*] Done to death by sland'rous tongues
                    Was Regina who here lies.
              Wrench the heart and burst the lungs
                    Telling of the harsh surprise.
              Lack-a-day, Regina's gone,   5
                    Dark the night and bleak the dawn.

                       Enter CADY HERON.

CADY   The sad report is mine to make, and I'm
              Asham'd to say the truth, which cometh with
              Regret and grief: 'tis how death came to her.

STUDENTS   [*singing:*] For the which, with songs of woe,   10
                    We sing out our mournful song.
              Round about her tomb we go,
                    Sadder than the day is long.
              Lack-a-day, Regina's gone,
                    Dark the night and bleak the dawn.   15
                                              [*Exeunt students.*

CADY   Nay, 'tis a jest, Regina did not die!
              She hath been hurt, indeed, but not to death.
              The rumors swirl'd an 'twere Charybdis' pool,
              With strength to pull in any who drew near.
              'Twas said her head did turn completely 'round,   20

As if it were the earth, her neck its axis.
'Twas said I push'd her in the path of harm,
Which were foul words far worse than any other.

Enter LADY HERON *and* SIR HERON, *in their residence.*
CADY *sits at a table with them.*

LADY H.	Hast thou no stomach for this supper, Cady?
	Mayhap thy conscience overwhelms thy belly.
CADY	Nay, Mother, prithee: I am not to blame.
LADY H.	Forsooth, I know not what I should believe.
CADY	If thou dost seek a cause for thy belief,
	Believe in me, thy humble daughter true.
	I should be testament and proof enow
	To satisfy thine anxious unbelief.

                     [Lady Heron begins putting dishes away.

LADY H.	Canst thou, my daughter faithful, say wherefore
	My tribal vases hide beneath the sink,
	As if they shirk'd in shame at some foul deed?
CADY	Beg pardon, Mother?
LADY H.	—Wilt thou play one scene
	Of excellent dissembling, let it look
	Like perfect honor? These, my precious vases:
	Why were they here conceal'd beneath the sink?
CADY	[*aside:*] I know, but shall not say. [*To Lady Heron:*]
	I do not know.
LADY H.	These are the vases of fertility
	Of the magnificent Ndebele tribe.
	They priceless are, and irreplaceable.
	Doth this mean anything to thee? Pray tell!
CADY	Nay, little. Less than none.

Line numbers: 25, 30, 35, 40

LADY H.   —What hath befallen?
          Who art thou? Verily, I know thee not.   45
                              [*Exit Lady Heron.*

CADY   This is the perfect end to fortune's fall:
          My friends despise me. Now my mother, too.

SIR H.   Thy mother doth not, could not thee despise.
          She is afeard of how thou dost mature.
          We, peradventure, err'd with actions swift,   50
          Too quickly enter'd thee in mainstream schooling.
          Belike returning home for school once more
          Would give thee space thou needest to be whole.

CADY   Nay, though for mercy I do thank thee, Father.
          'Twould be e'en worse to hide myself from school   55
          Than to return and face what I have done.

SIR H.   How bad a situation shall it be
          When thou again arrivest on the morrow?

CADY   Dost thou remember when, in Africa,
          We saw some lions fighting angrily   60
          O'er one small carcass of a warthog slain?
          I'll warrant 'twill be I who is the warthog.

SIR H.   My daughter is no warthog. Thou art lion—
          O thou art woman, I can hear thee roar.

CADY   O Father kind, thy discourse serves to make me   65
          Determin'd to achieve my final goal.

SIR H.   Give focus to thy studies for a while.
          Thou still, in classes, art superior,
          Is this not true?

CADY   —Alas, there's one thing more.
          My mathematics test, for calculus,   70
          Thou must inscribe thy signature withal.

SIR H.   Yet wherefore?

CADY	—I am failing in the class.
SIR H.	Ah, 'tis a problem I cannot o'erlook.
	Thou art—what is the word? Thou grounded art.
CADY	I like it not, but do accept the sentence. 75

[Exit Sir Heron. Cady walks to school.

Next, school I must endure, with frightful nerves.

Enter JANIS IAN, DAMIAN, *and other* STUDENTS.
CADY *finds that her desk has been removed.*

DAMIAN	Alas, a lass can find no seat—alas.
CADY	[*aside:*] My desk is ta'en, for they are mad at me.
	Behind the student flatulent I'll sit,
	Though it may cost my nostrils and my pride. 80

*[The gassy student releases
a swift squeak of flatulence.*

GASSY STD.	[*aside:*] This Cady hath become the school's pariah.
	My derrière shall put her in her place.
	This is a sweet revenge, though not so sweet.

*[The bell rings. Exeunt all students except Cady,
who walks to her next class.*

CADY	[*aside:*] How shameful and disgraceful is this day—
	At luncheon, ev'ry eye was fix'd on me. 85
	E'en as the volume of the din decreas'd,
	I heard a voice exclaim, "There is the one—
	She who did shove Regina 'fore the bus!"
	Another whisper'd, "Didst thou see the deed?"
	The many there were hungrier for gossip 90
	Than for the lunches that before them sat.
	No table held a place of refuge for me.
	Instead, as on the day I first arriv'd,

I found a lonely dining place within
The stalls inside the women's restroom. O,   95
This sad, long loneliness doth sour this day.

Enter SIR DUVALL *and two* POLICEMEN.
Enter AARON SAMUELS *and other* STUDENTS *in mathematics class.*

DUVALL   Take heed, ye class of Madam Norbury,
                We have some inquiries to ask of ye:
                Has e'er your teacher tried to sell or give
                You marijuana for a pastime smoke,   100
                Or tablets made of ecstasy's mystique?

STUD. 23   Nay, never.

STUD. 24   —What are marijuana tablets?
                                        [Cady arrives at her seat.

CADY   [*to Aaron:*] What doth unfold? Where's Madam
                                        Norbury?

AARON   [*to Sir Duvall:*] Good Sir Duvall, this is ridiculous—
                An errant search to find a phantom crime.   105
                Kind Madam Norbury ne'er selleth drugs.

DUVALL   Inside my heart I know 'tis true, indeed.
                Yet after ev'ry allegation 'gainst
                Coach Carr did prove to be extremely true,
                The school board hath insisted ev'ry claim   110
                Within the pages of the wretched book
                Shall forthwith be investigated, Aaron.

AARON   'Twas written by a scorn of silly lasses—
                Which, like a pride of lions, leap of salmon,
                A romp of otters, prickle form'd by hedgehogs, 115
                A plump of seals, a squabble made of seagulls—
                Most aptly doth describe their greatest feature.

These lasses spend their time devising rumors
Whilst facing all the boredom of their lives.

DUVALL   A noble speech and proper, Aaron, yet   120
Unless an individual comes forth
And doth declare, "'Tis I who am to blame!
The fiction of the book was my creation!"
We must continue in this rigid way.

CADY   [*aside:*] This wrong I must make right, and bid
farewell 125
To Aaron, who shall hate me when 'tis done.
[*To Sir Duvall:*] I do beseech ye, Sir Duvall: 'twas I.
The book was writ by my deceitful hand.

DUVALL   My disappointment knows no bound or limit.
Come, Cady, we must take thee hence away,   130
Brave punishments I shall devise for thee.
[Exeunt Cady, Sir Duvall, and policemen.

AARON   [*aside:*] So sweet was ne'er so fatal. I must weep,
But they're cruel tears: this sorrow's heavenly;
It strikes where it doth love. O, Cady dear,
Thou ever wert so generous and kind,   135
Yet can it be that thou didst instigate
The atmosphere of hatefulness that hath,
These many days, been plaguing North Shore High?
Thine actions are a tribute to thy spite—
Confession, though, hath help'd thee walk aright.   140
[Exeunt Aaron and other students.

SCENE 2

*At the George residence, North Shore High School,
and the Mathletes competition.*

Enter CADY HERON, *holding flowers.*
Enter REGINA GEORGE *in bed wearing a neck brace,* LADY GEORGE,
and several FRIENDS *surrounding* REGINA, *aside.*

CADY   Though angry at Regina, ne'ertheless,
            Beginning of my penitence is she—
            Let this reveal how my remorse persisted.

                   [Cady enters Regina's room
                   and hands her flowers.

REGINA   Though I am hurt, I do accept thy gift,
            And thy profound apologies withal.   5

               [Exeunt Regina, Lady George, and friends.
                   Cady walks to school.

CADY   When one is bitten by a vicious snake,
            The poison must at once extracted be.
            So I must suck the poison from my life.
            The gathering of friends around Regina
            Doth prove the more that folk are scar'd of thee, 10
            The more delug'd in flowers shalt thou be.
            The bigger task is Madam Norbury,
            Who proves that no good deed unpunish'd is.

Enter MADAM NORBURY, AARON SAMUELS,
KEVIN GNAPOOR, *and other* STUDENTS *in math class.*

NORBURY   Miss Heron, how delightful to see thee.
           I have a vent'rous fairy that shall seek   15
           The dealer's hoard and fetch thee some new drugs.
CADY   I have completed my examination.
NORBURY   Stay thou a moment, I shall grade it now.
                         [Madam Norbury begins grading the test.
                              Aaron stands aside, listening.
           Methinks that watching whilst my house was search'd
           By constables from ev'ry precinct near   20
           Did serve as perfect cherry on the top
           Of tasteless cake that is this blessèd year.
           Art thou in trouble grave for telling true,
           Confessing to the Burn Book thou didst write?
CADY   'Twas trouble most severe.
NORBURY   —I know one thing: 25
           Thou hast not author'd ev'ry word alone.
           Didst thou tell Sir Duvall the other names,
           Coauthors and accomplices of thine?
CADY   Nay, Madam Norbury, for I explore
           New paths by which I may comport myself—   30
           No more to speak of folk behind their backs.
                              [Aaron comes forward.
AARON   Indeed, for to be stricken by a bus
           Is punishment enow for knavery.
NORBURY   Thy grade is ninety-four, familiar soul.
AARON   Nerd, thou art welcome back to math with us.   35
CADY   My thanks. [*To Madam Norbury:*] To you, wise
                                        Madam Norbury,
           I make apology with humblest heart.
NORBURY   Thou art forgiven. Yet, as punishment,
           I have decided how thou shalt secure

The extra credit thou so deeply wanted.   40

> [*Kevin comes forward.*
> *Exeunt Madam Norbury, Aaron, and*
> *all students except Cady and Kevin.*

KEVIN   Behold, young Africa, together we
Shall plot coordinates of a success.
Here is thy tunic—thou art Mathlete proud,
And in our competition shall serve well.
The bank of students who contend this year   45
Shall prove most excellent combatants, yet
Will never match the prowess of our team.

Enter TIM PAK *and other* STUDENTS *on the North Shore Mathlete team.*
They venture to the Mathlete competition. Enter the MARYMOUNT
MATHLETE TEAM, *the* HOST, *and a few* SPECTATORS.

NORBURY   Good team, in all your skill do I believe—
Go forward into battle proudly, troops.

KEVIN   Ye whoresons, Marymount! Ye shall be crush'd!   50
By any angle we shall dominate.

NORBURY   [*to Cady:*] Art thou chock-full of nerves?

CADY   —Indeed I am.

NORBURY   Be not concern'd, I'll wager thou shalt thrive.
Naught is there to disrupt thy focus here—
Not one among those lads of Marymount   55
Could be describ'd as cute or fair or handsome.

HOST   Good evening, gentleladies, gentlemen.
Ye are most welcome to the Illinois
State Mathlete High School Championship.

AUDIENCE   —Huzzah!

HOST   The competition shall begin with this   60

First question of this thrilling evening: twice
The larger of two numbers is three more
That five times that which smaller is. The sum
Of four times that which larger is and three
Times of the smaller comes to sev'nty-one.   65
What are the numbers which we seek herein?

                                          [A buzzer sounds.

North Shore, have ye solv'd it?

KEVIN	—Fourteen and five.
HOST	Correct. Proceed we unto question two.

An odd three-digit number ye must find
Whose digits add up to the number twelve.   70
Each digit shall be diff'rent from the next—
The difference betwixt the first two digits
Is equal to the difference betwixt—

                                          [A buzzer sounds.

Now Marymount, ye have the answer found?

MARY. 1	'Tis seven hundred forty-one. Is't not? 75
HOST	Correct.
CADY	[*aside:*] —Fie, I am rusty at my math.

Enter LADY HERON *and* SIR HERON *above, on balcony.*

LADY H.	Hast thou seen Cady?
SIR H.	—She departed hence.
LADY H.	Didst thou not ground her? Was it not thy word?
SIR H.	Is this how grounding works? I do not know—
	She never once in Africa was grounded. 80
	'Tis practic'ly a foreign concept, dear.
	[*Aside:*] Are all ye groundlings grounded? Is that it?
LADY H.	At times, thy senselessness confoundeth me!

[Exeunt Lady Heron and Sir Heron.

CADY   [*aside:*] The competition doth go on and on—
         In troth, far longer than a play will bear.   85
         The globe of mathematics spinneth 'round—
         The stage is set to see the final match.

HOST   Full eighty-seven minutes have expir'd,
         And just as an equation ends with equals
         Our competition draweth to a tie.   90
         This tie doth bring a round of sudden death.
         Each team shall choose whom, from the other side,
         They shall confront as their opponent final.
         North Shore: whom dost thou choose from
                                              Marymount?

KEVIN   We shall select the lass, contestant Krafft.   95
HOST   From Marymount, Miss Caroline of Krafft.
MARY. 1 We, too, shall choose the lass, of minds the least.
HOST   From North Shore High, Miss Caddy Heron 'tis.
CADY   Fie, Cady 'tis—shall no one speak it right?
         Alas, the words do strike me suddenly—   100
         'Tis I who must my North Shore represent.

KEVIN   All confidence have I in thee, smart Afric—
         The mathematics and the metaphysics,
         Fall to them as thou find'st thy stomach serves thee.
                       [Cady and Caroline take center stage,
                                facing off against each other.

CADY   [*aside:*] This Caroline of Krafft hath eyebrows full—   105
         Full like the mane upon a horse's neck.
         My pluck I show by thinking she should pluck!
         Her outfit—hath it come from Sunday school?
         Old-fashion'd an 'twere chosen by the blind.
         Her cheap lip gloss hides not her snaggletooth,   110

	Which lurks, like shark behind a rock, to strike.
	Alas—what am I doing? Why these thoughts?
	Too much do I abuse this Car'line Krafft!
	My slander shall not stop her beating me—
HOST	In faith, distraction may yet be my downfall. 115

HOST   You two contestants, find the limit of
This math equation I shall show to ye.

[An equation appears on a screen.

CADY   [*aside:*] To call a person fat makes one not thinner,
To call a person dumb makes one not smarter,
To hurt Regina gave me no delight—   120
One must but solve the problem 'fore one's eyes,
Each day has trouble plenty of its own.

[A buzzer sounds.

CAROLINE   The limit! It is negative one, yea?

CADY   [*aside:*] Alas! She hath the answer. I have lost.

HOST   Nay, 'tis not so. The answer's incorrect.   125
We are, I do repeat, in sudden death—
If now Miss Heron can the answer give,
It shall be North Shore High School that prevails.

CADY   [*aside:*] By limits wherefore am I limited?
How doth the information 'scape my mind?   130
A-ha! 'Twas on the day when Aaron's hair
Was newly shorn, an 'twere a new-plough'd field.
How handsome was he then! Yet, Cady, focus—
What was upon the board past Aaron's head?
If limits ne'er approach to anything,   135
The limits, then, do not exist. 'Tis it!
[*To host:*] The limit, then, doth not exist!

HOST   —Correct.
Our new state champions, the North Shore Mathletes!

        [Cady and Caroline shake hands.

KEVIN   What of it, Marymount? You have been topp'd!

             Our sum is greater than our single parts!   140

             How like ye now the Kevin of North Shore?

             I prithee get some Kevin while he lasts!

                   [Exeunt Marymount students, Host, and
                  audience. Cady, Kevin, and other North Shore
                      Mathletes don their new doublets.

TIM   Thou chos'st the leather sleeves—the finest cut!

KEVIN   Thou didst it, Afric—thou solution perfect!

CADY   My thanks.

                  [Kevin hands Madam Norbury a doublet.

NORBURY   —K. G., thou hast my gratitude.   145

KEVIN   Imagine, then, how well we all shall look

             When, straighter than a keen hypotenuse,

             We roll to Fling of Spring with doublets new!

CADY   Alas, I may not go.

TIM   —What dost thou mean?

KEVIN   This is thy night, good Cady—thou deserv'st it.   150

             Thy reputation may be variable,

             Yet let thou not the haters win the day

             Or stop thee from expressing thy good thang.

CADY   Didst thou say thang? What is this thang, I pray?

NORBURY   Nay, do not reprimand thyself fore'er.   155

CADY   I grounded am.

NORBURY   —Thou art already out;

             No grounding can thine aspiration flout.

                            [Exeunt.

SCENE 3

At North Shore High School.

Enter REGINA GEORGE, *dressing*
for the Fling of Spring, with LADY GEORGE.

LADY G.   Your face, my daughter, is a book where men
        May read strange matters. To beguile the time,
        Look like the time; bear welcome in your eye,
        Your hand, your tongue: look like the inn'cent flower,
        But be the serpent under it. So shalt   5
        Thou be the Fling of Spring queen as thou shouldst.

REGINA   I am as regal as befits a queen,
        Though crown'd by neck brace rather than pure gold.
        Be gentle, Mother, ere thou hurt'st me more.

Enter GRETCHEN WIENERS, *aside, dressing for the Fling of Spring.*

GRETCHEN   This hair, this dress, this necklace—each piece shall   10
        Conceal me what I am, and be my aid
        For such disguise as haply shall become
        The form of my intent. I shall succeed—
        Plain Gretchen by the day, by night a queen.

Enter KAREN SMITH, *aside, dressing for the Fling of Spring*
in front of a mirror.

KAREN   A perfect K form'd on my perfect chest,   15
        Of diamonds made, in sparkling glory shines.

I strive not to be queen of Fling of Spring—
It is an honor that I dream not of—
Yet I shall be a faithful courtesan.

> *[Karen turns from the mirror,*
> *revealing that the K is backward.*

Enter JANIS IAN *and* DAMIAN, *dressing for the Fling of Spring.*

DAMIAN   Tuxedos made of purple cloth are ours—   20
            Imperial in hue, like Rome of old.
JANIS   We two, like twins, shall grace the Fling of Spring—
            Thou Romulus, I Remus, we shall reign.

> *[Regina, Lady George, Gretchen, Karen, Janis,*
> *and Damian converge at Fling of Spring.*

Enter AARON SAMUELS, SHANE OMAN, SIR DUVALL, *and many other*
STUDENTS *and* TEACHERS *at the Fling of Spring.*

DAMIAN   Forget not, ev'ryone, to cast your votes
            For who'll be queen and king of Fling of Spring!   25
            The dismal court of popularity
            Shall represent ye for the coming year.
            It is your civic duty, by my troth!
STUD. 25   Methinks I shall vote for Regina George,
            Who was unfairly wallop'd by a bus.   30
STUD. 26   Yet Cady Heron is my ballot's choice,
            For she did push Regina valiantly.
SHANE   Come, sweet Regina, let us stand and pose
            To make a portrait for posterity.

> *[Regina and Shane pose to have their*
> *photograph taken.*

LADY G.   [*aside:*] A moment pure, a couple purer still!   35
            I cannot help but in the background stand,
            That I may take my place in history.

            Enter LADY HERON *and* SIR HERON.
               They approach SIR DUVALL.

LADY H.   Have you seen Cady Heron, Sir Duvall?
            She should be grounded, but my doltish husband
            Releas'd her from our presence by mistake.   40
SIR H.   I did not know! Do you know "grounding," sir?
DUVALL   Young Cady is not here; I've seen her not.
            Behold! She cometh with the Mathlete team.

            Enter CADY HERON, MADAM NORBURY,
        KEVIN GNAPOOR, TIM PAK, *and other Mathlete*
            STUDENTS. SIR DUVALL *mounts the stage.*

            [*To all:*] Now 'tis the time to gather nominees
            For queen and king of Fling of Spring on stage.   45
                [Regina, Janis, Gretchen, Shane, and three other
                            lads join Sir Duvall on the stage.
            Ere I announce, hear this: you all are winners,
            E'en ye who lose are winners in your hearts.
            I could not gladder be that this year endeth,
            And with it all the challenges therein.
            Now to the prize: the Fling of Spring king is   50
            Shane Oman.
                                        [*All applaud.*
SHANE   —Ha! My proper recompense!
            For sans a doubt I am most kingly, yea,

	King of all I survey throughout the school!	
LADY H.	I'll signal Cady—she must hither come	
	And face our wrath for not remaining grounded.	55
DUVALL	Your Fling of Spring queen—future cochair of	
	The board of student-led activities,	
	And winner of two gift certificates	
	Unto the Walker Brothers Pancake House—	
	Is Cady Heron.	
LADY H.	—What? My precious lass?	60

[All applaud.

| DUVALL | Where, then, is Cady? I did spy her once. | |
| | Ah, now I see her. Join me on the stage. | |

[Cady mounts the stage.
Sir Duvall places a crown on her head.

CADY	You have my thanks—this meaneth much to me,	
	You have my disbelief and wonder, too.	
DUVALL	'Tis not requir'd that thou shalt speechify.	65
CADY	I am near finish'd, sir, you have my word.	
	Half of the students in this room are angry—	
	Upset at me and all the things I've done.	
	The other only like me for the rumor	
	That I push'd someone in a busly path.	70
	In neither case doth this sit well with me.	
	To all the people who were damag'd by	
	The Burn Book and its contents horrible,	
	I am so sorry—more than you can know.	

[Cady removes her crown.

	Ne'er in my life have I attended such	75
	A fanciful event as Fling of Spring.	
	When I bethink me how this honor was	
	Desir'd and treasur'd by so many here,	

How many tears were spill'd o'er what it means,
I wholly am bereft. For look around,   80
How lucky we are to be alive right now—
Each person here is dress'd like royalty.
See Jessica Lopez, with dress astounding—
Of orange hue, amazing to observe.
Good Emma Gerber there, thy hair is fine,   85
Undoubtedly it took thee hours to style
And thou dost brighter shine than ev'ry star.
Why are we, then, distress'd about this token?
It is mere plastic, which doth eas'ly break.

> [*Cady breaks her crown into pieces.*

DAMIAN   Alas, to see it break doth rend my heart!   90
CADY   What if we shar'd the honor, all of us?

> [*Cady begins throwing pieces
> of the crown to others.*

A piece for Gretchen Wieners, earnest lass,
A partial queen of Fling of Spring most charming.
A piece for Janis Ian, friend most true.
DUVALL   Most people take the crown and leave the stage.   95
CADY   A piece, as well, for our Regina George,
Who spine was fractur'd, yet she gloweth still.
More, too, for all the other lasses here—
Each one of you a spirit beautiful.

> [*All applaud as Cady continues
> throwing pieces of the crown.*

LADY H.   [*aside:*] How can a mother's angriness endure   100
When pride o'erwhelmeth anger in her heart?
CADY   By heaven, Sir Duvall, has this not gone
On long enow? Pray, end the ceremony.
DUVALL   Ha, ha! Thou hast done admirably, Cady.

	Enjoy yourselves, you young ones. Strike up, pipers! 105
	[All students descend from the stage to dance.
JANIS	[*to Damian:*] Behold, I am a queen, with crown to
	prove't!
DAMIAN	I also am!
CADY	[*approaching:*] —Holla, my friends.
JANIS	—Holla.
CADY	Are we still fighting, or shall truce be call'd?
JANIS	Art thou still ass-like, or be callèd kind?
CADY	My days of assery I leave behind. 110
JANIS	My days of fighting thee I leave as well.
DAMIAN	This song that plays—I love it, yea, I do!
JANIS	This song that plays—I hate it, yea, I do!
CADY	This song that plays—I know it, yea, I do!
DAMIAN	Behind thee, Cady, comes man candy hither. 115

*[Aaron approaches. Janis and Damian turn
away to give Cady privacy.*

CADY   Good even, Aaron.

AARON   —By my troth, I thought
Thou wouldst not make it to the Fling of Spring.

[He pulls certificates from his pocket.

As agent of the seniors, 'tis my spot
To thee two gift certificates to bring.

[Janis and Damian grab one gift certificate.

JANIS   My thanks, thou jester!

DAMIAN   —Sooth, we fly like fairies!   120

AARON   'Tis then a single gift certificate
Unto the Walker Brothers Pancake House.

CADY   My thanks, sweet Aaron. I shall treasure it.

[They begin to dance.

AARON   Congratulations on thy win, sweet mouse—
I hear the Mathletes beat the state entire.   125

CADY   How nervous was I! Limits near did end me.
Indeed, methought some vomit might transpire.

AARON   How is thy stomach? Say if I should fend me.

CADY   It feeleth fine.

AARON   —Not e'en the smallest grumble?
An thou art nauseous, wilt tell me so?   130

CADY   Indeed.

AARON   —No drinking, neither?

CADY   —I'll not stumble.

AARON   Then all is grool—I fear no greater woe.

[They kiss. Aside, Janis and Damian dance.

JANIS   Shall we endeavor kissing, as they do?

[Janis and Damian kiss.

DAMIAN   Foul, foul!

JANIS   —'Twas a profound mistake!

DAMIAN   —Forsooth!

[Exit Damian. Kevin approaches Janis.

KEVIN   Where one departs, another takes its place—   135

This fraction is mine opportunity.

JANIS   May I help thee?

KEVIN   —Art thou, lass, Puerto Rican?

The island hath a quotient of my soul.

JANIS   Nay, Lebanese.

KEVIN   —I feel that in my bones—

A function of my reverence for thee.   140

[All freeze as Cady comes forward.

CADY   Our tale concludeth for the present moment.

Yet, ere we go, we'll tell the futures of

The characters ye witness'd in our play.

The Plastics were disbanded, happily,

A mercy for the school and for each one.   145

Regina's spine did heal from tip to tip.

Her therapist help'd her to channel rage

By playing contact sports with eager will.

'Twas perfect, for the jock girls lov'd her so,

Were not afeard of her great vehemence.   150

Meanwhile, sweet Karen us'd her talent rare

To make prognostication of the weather.

Each morning she could tell the town entire—

By using the two sensors on her chest—

The temp'rature and likeliness of rain.   155

Kind Gretchen found herself another clique,

A new queen bee to serve and praise withal—

Wherein her vast Korean language skills

Were treasur'd by her newfound Asian friends.

Mine Aaron went to university—   160
Northwestern, near enow that I may see him
When swiftly run the days from week to weekend.
And last, I went from homeschool'd jungle freak
To shiny Plastic—fake and terrible—
To the most-hated person in the school,   165
To, finally, a normal human soul.
Our Janis and her Kevin were as one,
And ev'rything was happily resolv'd.
The drama of the year did pass us by
And seem'd not so important in the next.   170
Once, school was like a shark tank, baring teeth,
Yet now 'tis simpler, letting us each float.
Girl World hath found a peace within itself.
And though the Junior Plastics did arrive,
Repeating the mistakes we once did make,   175
A solid bus careening through the street
Shall set them in their place most ardently.
Nay, 'tis not so—I purely am in jest.
Although the world, like tempest, 'round us whirls,
We dwell in peace, no more to be mean girls.   180

[Exeunt omnes.

END.

AFTERWORD

The story of Cady, her friends, and her frenemies is deserving of a Shakespearean treatment—a tale of how relationships are broken by misunderstanding and repaired by circumstance and humility. William Shakespeare's female characters were never as strong as those of Tina Fey's creation, which is why I had so much fun giving the Bard a dose of feminism in *William Shakespeare's Much Ado About Mean Girls*. Writing this book has been an absolute joy. I only hope I have done the movie justice.

A note about the staging: The film *Mean Girls* jumps freely from scene to scene, often in short clips that make a joke or emphasize a point. On Shakespeare's stage such quick flashes would have been almost unknown, so I improvised. Characters enter and exit the balcony quickly, and brief cinematic scenes spanning multiple days and locations are tied together in a single theatrical scene. For example, in Act III, scene 2, Damian finds the Kälteen bars in Cady's satchel that he had just pretended to steal, whereas the movie switches to a separate scene in Cady's home. The final scenes of the film alternate frequently between the Mathlete competition and Spring Fling; I have rearranged these into two distinct scenes. Finally, because Cady's voice so often narrates the film, in my adaptation she has more asides than Shakespearean characters ever would.

This is my first Shakespearean adaptation outside the action/sci-fi genre and my first adaptation of a story centered on the lives of women. I decided to try something I had never done before. Instead of including Shakespearean references at whim, whenever and wherever they occurred to me, I paired each main female character in *Mean Girls* with a Shakespearean counterpart. In other words, each Shakespearean reference is taken from a specific Shakespearean character. These are the characters I paired together:

- Cady: Miranda in *The Tempest*. Miranda is an ingenue who has lived most of her life secluded with her father in a remote wilderness, not unlike Cady. (I broke this pairing once, when Cady uses lines borrowed from Hero in *Much Ado About Nothing*. The quote from Hero was so perfect for the moment that I had to use it. Can you find it?)

- Janis: Beatrice in *Much Ado About Nothing*. Beatrice has a caustic, biting wit and a fierce loyalty to her friends.

- Regina: Kate in *Taming of the Shrew*. Kate, the titular shrew, starts off the play as a harsh woman with a sharp tongue.

- Gretchen: Viola in *Twelfth Night*. Viola, dressing as a man, serves as a constant go-between and wears a different face with each character.

- Karen: Juliet in *Romeo and Juliet*. Juliet is the youngest of Shakespeare's heroines. She is innocent and hopeful.

- Mrs. Heron: Cleopatra in *Antony and Cleopatra*. Cleopatra is the regal, intelligent woman who has come from Africa.

- Mrs. George: Lady Macbeth in *Macbeth*. Lady Macbeth is one of Shakespeare's cruelest, most cunning villains. Yes, this is unfair to Amy Poehler's portrayal of Mrs. George, who is nothing but positive and fun. My thought was that anyone who could raise Regina must be a piece of work.

- Ms. Norbury: Titania in *A Midsummer Night's Dream*. There's little textual connection here—I just love Tina Fey so much that I thought, "Who could represent her except a majestic fairy queen?"

In addition to these references, you will likely notice other Shakespearean nods and conventions. After Cady and Aaron kiss for the first time, they begin speaking to each other in rhyming quatrains, like Romeo and Juliet. Kevin Gnapoor, the adorable badass deejay and math geek, uses a mathematical term every time he opens his mouth.

Thanks for reading, friends. Go forth and be your amazing selves. And watch out for buses.

ACKNOWLEDGMENTS

Thank you to every woman who has made my life a little bit better:

My spouse and best friend, Jennifer Creswell.

My mother, Beth Doescher.

My mother-in-law, Caryl Creswell.

My sisters-in-law, Katherine Creswell, Em Doescher, and Sibyl Siegfried.

My nieces, Aracelli, Addison, and Sophie.

My friends and family: Chloe Ackerman, Heidi Altman, Erin Buehler, Melody Burton, Emily Carminati, Jeanette Ehmke, Kristin Gordon, Marian Hammond, Holly Havens, Mona Havens, Nancy Hicks, Ruby Hicks, Anne Huebsch, Apricot Irving, Alexis Kaushansky, Rebecca Lessem, Andrea Martin, Joan Miller, Tara Morrill, Lucy Neary, Julia Rodriguez-O'Donnell, Helga and Isabella Scott, Sarah Shepherd, Naomi Walcott, Nicole, Mackinzie, Audrey, and Lily Warne-McGraw, Katie Wire, and Sarah Woodburn. Thank you, also, to many of their spouses.

My teachers Jane Bidwell, Betsy Deines, Doree Jarboe, Chris Knab, and Janice Morgan.

Thank you to the team at Quirk Books: my editor Jhanteigh Kupihea (our first project together!), Nicole De Jackmo, Kelsey Hoffman, Jane Morley, Christina Schillaci, Ivy Weir, Rick Chillot, Brett Cohen, Andie Reid, and the rest of the crew.

To my boys, Liam and Graham—boys who are, hopefully, growing to be good men.

You don't need to be a Shakespeare scholar to enjoy *William Shakespeare's Much Ado About Mean Girls*. But if you've come to this book with more knowledge about Plastics than playwrights, this reader's guide may help deepen your understanding of the language and structure of the book, all of which is inspired by Shakespeare's work.

Iambic Pentameter

Shakespeare wrote his plays in a specific syllabic pattern known as iambic pentameter. An *iamb* is a unit of meter, sometimes called a foot, consisting of two syllables, the first of which is unstressed, or soft, and the second of which is stressed, or emphasized. Together the two syllables of an iamb sound like "da-DUM," as in beyond ("be-YOND"), across ("a-CROSS"), and Duvall ("du-VALL"). *Pentameter* is a line of verse containing five feet. So iambic pentameter consists of five iambs, or ten syllables alternating in emphasis. A famous example of this meter, with the stressed half of each iamb in bold, is:

I'd **rath**er **be** a **ham**mer **than** a **nail**.

However, Shakespeare broke the rule almost as much as he observed it. The most famous Shakespearean line of all has eleven syllables, not ten: "To **be** or **not** to **be**, that **is** the **quest**ion." That last *-ion* is known as a weak ending, or an unstressed syllable. Shakespeare often used weak endings, added two unstressed syllables where there should be one, and left out syllables.

Let's see iambic pentameter in action with this speech from Act I, scene 2 (see page 34).

JANIS   What fire is in mine ears? What scene was this?
         No glory lives behind the back of such.   255
         The Plastics say thou dost deserve, and I
         Believe it better than reportingly.
         Thou hast been claim'd and thou shalt take thy claim!
         Thou shalt wear pink upon the morrow, yea,
         And make report of all Regina sayeth,   260
         No matter how horrendous, rank, and vile.

If you read this speech aloud, you may notice that the dialogue sounds unnatural if spoken according to how the individual lines are broken. Rather, punctuation should guide how lines of iambic pentameter are spoken, as if the speech were written as prose. Consider lines 256–257: "The Plastics say thou dost deserve, and I / Believe it better than reportingly." This sentence—which contains language borrowed from Shakespeare's *Much Ado About Nothing*—is split across two lines. When read, the lines should naturally flow into the next. (By the way, line 260 in this speech contains an example of a weak ending.)

What about words with more than two syllables? The trick with multisyllabic words is to figure out which syllable in the word has the primary emphasis. Let's consider the word *calamity* (as in P. J. Calamity's): The primary emphasis is normally on the second syllable, calamity. In iambic pentameter, it makes sense to pronounce it as two iambs, "cala-" and "-mity." The final syllable -*ty* provides a secondary stress that fits the meter nicely.

Other Shakespearean Hallmarks

The following features of a Shakespearean play are all found in *William Shakespeare's Much Ado About Mean Girls.*

- **Five acts.** Plays in Shakespeare's time were structured in five parts, drawing on the tradition of ancient Roman plays. Acts can contain any number of scenes.
- **Minimal stage directions.** Shakespeare left it to the performers to determine who should do what on stage. I tried to do the same when writing *William Shakespeare's Much Ado About Mean Girls*, but this play has far more stage directions than one of Shakespeare's would, to ensure that sequences are clear. Shakespeare never had his characters dance to a skipping CD player, after all.
- **Rhyming couplets at the end of scenes.** A rhyming couplet is a pair of consecutive lines ending with a similar sound. For example, Act II, scene 1, lines 99–100 (see page 52): "Anon I'll tell my friends what I have seen— / This Burn Book tactless, fill'd with spirit mean." Shakespeare ended his scenes this way to indicate a narrative shift to the audience, similar to a final cadence in music.
- **Asides.** An aside is dialogue that the audience can hear but that the characters other than the speaker do not. These speeches often explain a character's motivations or inner thoughts or reveal background information to the audience. We might also describe this as a character "breaking the fourth wall," that is, crossing the imaginary divide between stage and audience to address the spectators directly.
- **Soliloquies.** These monologues are similar to asides in that often they explain a character's behavior or motivation. But

they occur when the character is alone on stage and tend to be longer than asides.

- **Anaphora.** Anaphora is the repetition of a word or phrase at the start of successive lines, used for rhetorical effect. Damian employs anaphora in Act I, scene 2, lines 296–299 (see page 36), where he starts several lines with the phrase "Pink is." (A similar speech appears in Shakespeare's *Henry the Sixth, Part 1*, Act II, scene 4, lines 11–15.)

- **Stichomythia.** In stichomythia, characters exchange lines of dialogue back and forth, echoing and repeating one another. An example of stichomythia appears in the final reconciliation scene among Cady, Janis, and Damian in Act V, scene 3, lines 108–114 (see page 164). A similar exchange appears in Shakespeare's *Hamlet*, Act III, scene 4, lines 9–12.

- **Extended metaphors.** Shakespeare often draws out a metaphor in order to squeeze as much life from it as possible. One example is when Romeo and Juliet first meet and kiss in Act I, scene 5, of *Romeo and Juliet*; they make references to religion as an extended religious metaphor for their divine, nearly sacred love. Similarly, I used war as a metaphor in Act III, scene 5, lines 238–245 (see page 115), when Cady discusses her schemes.

- **Songs.** Shakespeare's plays are full of songs! Sometimes playful, sometimes mystical, sometimes sorrowful, songs appear at unexpected moments and often break the rhythm of iambic pentameter. *William Shakespeare's Much Ado About Mean Girls* includes multiple songs adapted from the film's soundtrack. An excerpt of my Shakespearean version of "Jingle Bell Rock" appears on pages 81–82.

SONNET G14

The web is so fetch . . .

Young Cady hath a newfound peace of mind,
The Plastics are disbanded, by and by,
E'en once-enrag'd Regina hath grown kind,
And all is well once more at North Shore High.
The sun doth set on this, our merry scene,
Yet if ye would have more, we pray read on:
Pull up **quirkbooks.com** upon thy screen
And thou shalt reap rewards from dusk to dawn!
Say, do thy students need a Bard refresher?
Find thou, online, an ample **teacher's guide.**
Wouldst read an **interview with Ian Doescher?**
E'en on the website shalt thou be supplied.
If thine enjoyment thou wouldst gladly stretch,
Get thee unto the website—'twill be fetch!

quirkbooks.com/muchadoaboutmeangirls